SHOWDOWN ON MAIN STREET

The Preacher slid home the last cartridge. He snapped the .44's cylinder shut and slid the big gun back into its holster. Standing by himself in the middle of Main Street, he hardly seemed to be breathing. The distance that separated him from Stockburn and the deputies was not great.

He waited.

As if marching in time to some unheard rhythm, Stockburn's men descended from the porch and crossed into the street.

They stared at the lone figure confronting them as they formed a single line stretching from boardwalk to boardwalk.

The Preacher's hand moved ever so slightly nearer the staghorn grip of his pistol. Beneath the shading brim of his hat, his eyes narrowed. He moved to meet them.

The distance between the one and the seven closed. To thirty-five yards, then to thirty, twenty-five . . .

At twenty-three yards the deputy on the far right went for his gun . . .

Also by
Alan Dean Foster

ALIEN
CLASH OF THE TITANS
THE MAN WHO USED THE UNIVERSE
KRULL
OUTLAND
THE I INSIDE
THE MOMENT OF THE MAGICIAN
SPELLSINGER
THE HOUR OF THE GATE
THE DAY OF THE DISSONANCE
SHADOWKEEP
STARMAN

Published by
WARNER BOOKS

PALE RIDER

a novelization by
ALAN DEAN FOSTER,
based on the screenplay by
MICHAEL BUTLER & DENNIS SHRYACK

WARNER BOOKS

A Warner Communications Company

For Harry Moore and Smithee,
My two favorite preachers.
Whose methodology is somewhat more conventional.

I

They called Conway "Spider" for several reasons, the foremost being that he insisted on it, his real given name being less than suitable for his current occupation. Rumor had it his parents had dubbed him Percy, but there wasn't a man in California who'd dare say that to his face.

The nickname fit his movements as well as his personality. Fiftyish, small in stature but wiry as an Arapaho pony, he didn't so much dig into his claim as scuttle back and forth across it. While the majority of the other miners were content to work their Long Toms—the six-foot-long sluice boxes that lined Carbon Creek—or to sit patiently on the sandy banks and labor over their gold pans, Conway was in constant motion. One minute he'd be panning, the next he'd be using a shovel to dig up river gravel, and the third would find him scanning the larger rocks for signs of color. Burnt brown by the relentless Sierra sun, his hands and fingers flicked through the pieces of granite and schist that infested his pan. From time to time he would pause long enough to wave reassuringly in the direction of his two grown sons.

Conway could wave with one hand and continue panning with the other. Through this unique talent he had acquired a certain celebrity. Few men possessed both the strength of wrist and delicacy of touch to pan for gold with only one hand. Somehow Conway managed the difficult balancing act.

Used to be a time when he'd gladly demonstrate his special ability to newcomers in return for a meal. He hadn't been able to do so for quite a while now. Not because he was unwilling. Quite the contrary. But the sad fact of the matter was that there hadn't been any newcomers come to Carbon Canyon in several months. There was reason for this.

Word of what was happening in Carbon had filtered out, and those miners who might've been tempted by Carbon's undeniable potential had also heard about the Other Thing.

So they called Conway Spider, and the name stuck. He made sure it stuck, because in the mining towns that lined the western slope of the Sierra Nevada the way pearls decorated the neck of Lola Montez, a sourdough named Percy wouldn't be likely to live very long. A man can only survive so many fights, and Conway was several years the distaff side of fifty. So Spider he was and Spider he was glad to be.

Putting aside his pan for a moment, he fumbled in his kit until he found a tin cup, and dipped it into the creek. Even though winter was still weeks away, the icy snowmelt was still cold and refreshing. Best water in the world, Conway reflected, and if you happened to suck in a little gravel with it, well, maybe you'd get your gold that way.

The old miner chuckled, recalling the tale of the Chinaman's Revenge. Way it had come about, down in Placerville, was that several men had refused to pay up for a whole month's worth of laundry work by one respected Son of Heaven. Since the Chinese immigrants were not worthy of a sheriff's notice, unless they happened to be involved in a violent altercation with a white man, it was left to the one who'd been cheated to seek recompense in his own way. This the man named Chang had done, and while he never did get his money, he certainly had his revenge.

Somehow the rumor got started that the three deadbeats had been burying their gold beneath the outhouse on their claim, where none would think to look for it. So naturally a bunch of wild-eyed would-be thieves had snuck out there one night. They'd torn the place apart searching for the hidden lode. None of the three miners had been able to halt the assault, with the result that the disappointed and odoriferous invaders had only departed the following morning, leaving the owners of the claim to clean up the results of the unwanted excavation while clad in their ill-cleaned clothes.

A smoke would be nice about now, Conway mused, but you didn't smoke down on the creek. Smoking was purely an after-hours pleasure. Daylight was for panning and sluicing. The high mountains that enveloped the canyon shortened the days, and the light was too precious to waste on relaxation. Time enough for that after a man's work was done. Sit back for a smoke and your fortune might go tumbling past your propped-up feet, right down the creek. Placer mining was not an occupation for the lazy.

Not that hard work would automatically make you rich. Carbon Canyon still held out the promise of that first big strike. And promise there was in plenty, if not easy riches. There was plenty of color, and just enough dust to hold a man back from leaving. It was still virgin territory, untouched by

3

the forty-niners who'd picked up the easy gold a few years back. A man just had to persevere. You had to work your way through the upper layer of gravel to get to the paydirt beneath. Everyone knew that, which was why Carbon Canyon had attracted so many good folks on the heels of Conway's first find.

No new arrivals for some time now, though. Conway grunted, letting his gaze wander from the fast-flowing waters of the creek up to the nearby cluster of buildings.

It wasn't much of a community, but the promise was there, a different, but in its own way no less exhilarating promise than the kind the creek held. Already a few families had traded in their original tarpaper shanties and lean-tos for more solid structures of lath and log. People were setting up homes in place of camps. Smoke drifted skyward from several stovepipes as the womenfolk who'd followed their men westward bustled about their hard-won kitchens. Their presence was further proof of the incipient community's vitality. Women didn't settle in a mining camp unless they had thoughts of living there permanent. Their attitudes infected their husbands. It's easy for a man to move from one claim to another, but hard to abandon a home. Such thoughts made Conway remember his own wife, remember how he'd come to lose her, and how long ago it had been.

A deep rumbling that rose above the play of the creek and the stones forced him out of his melancholy. Frowning, he rose to stare downstream. Summer thunderstorms were common enough in these mountains, but it was a mite late in the year for one to boil up over the peaks, and he was danged if he could see a single cloud. Of course, a man could be enjoying his lunch under a clear, warm sky one minute only to find himself racing for cover the next from a deluge fit to

4

tweak Noah's beard. That was the way the weather was in the Sierras.

Somewhere a mockingbird trilled uncertainly. Two Stellar jays chased each other through pine branches. Again the rumble, louder this time and sustained. Not thunder. Something else. Though it *could* be thunder. Spider Conway prayed it was thunder as he put his pan aside and squinted downcanyon. Was that a cloud rising from the lower elevations, or creek mist? But creek mist manifested itself only in the early morning, when the sun was still below the mountaintops. It was midday now, long past the time when such climatic conjurations occurred.

Megan Wheeler heard the noise too. She turned to stare down the creek. Fifteen going on sixteen (some might've said fifteen going on twenty), Megan Wheeler was poised awkwardly between childhood and womanhood. She was blessed with a precocious beauty that reflected both the vibrant voluptuousness of her mother and the sleek good looks of her long absent father.

She was using both hands to carry the heavy water bucket. Some of the water sloshed out as she whirled to gaze down the canyon. The dog that had been trotting at her heels also paused to eye its mistress quizzically. It wouldn't be very big even when it was full-grown, an important fact which Megan had used to advantage when she'd argued with her mother about keeping the mutt. Like Megan, it was full of energy and curiosity, half dog and half puppy. It did not turn its gaze down the canyon, but the manner in which its ears perked up showed that it too heard the intensifying rumble.

Hull Barret was working his sluice in the shade of the huge granite boulder that marked the center of his claim. The small mountain stuck out into the creek, forcing the flow around its immovable base. While he was momentarily glad of the shade, Barret had cursed the huge monolith from the first day he'd begun panning. The big rock squatted right where he would've liked to have set up his Long Tom. Nothing to do about it but begin work elsewhere, though. It takes time and money to move mountains, even small ones. Barret had little of either. So the chunk of mountain stayed where it was, a constant taunt to his best efforts. He lavished what little time and as many curses as he could spare on its smooth sides.

There was concern on his face now as he let loose of the sluice rocker and moved slightly upslope to get a better view down the canyon. Hull Barret was thirty-five. Somehow he managed not to look any older despite a lifetime of doing everyone else's hard work. The latter was what had driven him all the way across the continent to California and eventually to Carbon Canyon. The work he was doing now was harder than ever, but for the first time in his life he didn't have to kiss the hem of anyone's shirttail or bow and scrape in return for a meager paycheck. He was his own master, like the other miners in the canyon. What little he wrung from the creek belonged to him and no one else.

By now all the inhabitants of the canyon were staring nervously downstream. A man would have to be deaf in order to be able to ignore the sound. It echoed off the canyon walls and rattled the few glass windows in the better-built cabins.

Conway dumped the contents of his pan on the ground and prepared to run for high ground. As he turned a gleam in the pile of discarded sand caught his eye. The nugget was tiny, barely bigger than a fleck, but a nugget it was. He bent to retrieve it, and felt the weight of it as it rested in his gnarled hand.

Now don't that just beat all, he thought, wondering why

the find failed to relieve his anxiety over the rising thunder. Apprehensively he pocketed the tiny lump and began to retreat in the direction of his cabin.

Abruptly the source of the noise hove into view. It was neither storm cloud nor one of the rare earthquakes that occasionally rattled this part of the Sierra. Nine, ten, a dozen horses and riders were pounding up the creekbed at full gallop toward the little community. Spray flew from hooves, creating the cloud that had intrigued Hull Barret. It caught the sun and shattered it into a thousand tiny rainbows just as the horsemen were destroying the peace of the midafternoon. The spray itself was beautiful, but neither miners nor kin thought of standing their ground to admire the transitory beauty.

"Goddamn!" Conway growled. His fingers clenched and opened helplessly as he watched the riders approach. Then he grabbed up his pan and gear and ran for his cabin.

Everyone was running; scrambling to recover mining equipment or personal effects, racing for shelter, just trying to get out of the invaders' path. They were full of despair, panic, and resignation. Disaster had befallen them, and the worst of it was they had come to expect it.

Not everyone was fleeing from the oncoming horsemen. A small spotted dog chose to stand his ground, barking with feeble ferocity at the far larger quadrupeds that were heading straight for him. As a race dogs are brave but not very bright.

"Linsey!" Megan Wheeler turned to scream at the pup. It ignored her, caught up by the overwhelming frenzy of the attack. Sharing with the dog a lack of maturity and common sense, Megan dropped the water bucket and raced downslope.

The horsemen began to spread out to cover both sides of the creek, firing their pistols into the air, yelling and hooting, and trying to do everything possible to add to the general

7

confusion and panic. They were not the sort of men one would invite to a genteel family function, and they were having themselves a high old time wreaking as much havoc as possible. They'd come to Carbon Canyon to have themselves a party. Only the locals weren't laughing.

Sarah Wheeler burst out of one of the older shanties set high up on the hillside and anxiously searched the confusion below. Her sharp blue eyes swept the slope, the creekbed, and the forest opposite without finding the figure they sought.

"Megan? Megan?" Her eyes widened and her face turned pale as she thought she saw a familiar shape darting about in the very thick of the havoc. No one turned to her. She couldn't make herself heard above the screams of men and women, the neighing of excited horses, and the echo of gunfire.

None of the many bullets found flesh, however. The visitors were not interested in murder. They'd come to batter the miners' spirits, not their bodies. A pity, too, some of the horsemen thought. There were so many easy targets, and of the best variety: the kind that don't fight back. Orders being orders, though, the gunmen restrained their natural impulses, aware that none of the dirtscrabblers now fleeing like sheep would ever think to thank them for exercising this forebearance.

They chased the retreating miners up the slopes until the grades grew too steep for horses if not panicky men. With the field cleared they turned their attention to the precious equipment that had been left behind. A single voice of defiance could be heard above the noise and disarray. It belonged to the only inhabitant of Carbon Canyon who still had the guts to offer some resistance, and it was a sad commentary that this voice belonged to a half-grown dog.

Not everyone ran all the way into the woods. Spider

Conway reached his shack and stopped there, unwilling to abondon his home. Hull Barret took up a position between his precious sluice box and the onrushing horde. He gripped a shovel in both hands and waited.

One rider came close. Barret swung, but the horse was moving too fast and the blow went awry. He overbalanced, was unable to correct for the swing, and went head over arse into the cold creek while the man he'd taken the swing at looked back and laughed.

The two horsemen following him simply ran over and through the Long Tom, pausing only long enough to ensure that their mounts' hooves smashed in the sides of the sluice and broke the wooden legs before riding on. Barret sat in the creek and looked on helplessly, holding tight to the useless shovel. There was nothing he could do, not a damn thing, and the knowledge of that helplessness was far more damaging to his enterprise than the ruined sluice could ever be.

One of the marauders chose to demonstrate his skill with the lariat. The pride he took in his effort was misplaced, since his target wasn't moving. It wasn't hard at all to get the loop around one of the supporting legs of a cabin while the other end was fastened to the saddlehorn. A few "gee-up's," a quick taste of the spur, and the man's horse did the real work. The support post pulled away cleanly, collapsing the cabin like a pile of cards. A solidly built structure wouldn't have suffered so, but like the majority of shelters in Carbon Canyon, this one had been put together more with hope and spit than with expensive nails and good wood. Even so, up until the rider had elected to exercise his cheap skill and bad humor, it had been somebody's home.

Now, like much of the invaluable mining equipment that

had been abandoned along the creek when the riders first arrived, it was a pile of garbage.

Sarah Wheeler stepped down off her porch and fought to focus on a single shape running in and out amidst the mass of horsemen. There was fear in her voice.

"Megan, no! Come back here, Megan!" She tried to run after her daughter and nearly darted into the path of an onrushing horse, pivoting to safety at the last possible second. Panting hard, she clung to the porch as the man who'd nearly run her down galloped through her clothesline, sending freshly laundered shirts and pinafores flying, trampling newly-scrubbed bloomers into the dirt.

The dog screamed then, the sound sharp and high pitched in the manner of dogs when they're surprised by an unexpected pain. Dogs and little children are convinced of their invulnerability and so pain always comes to them as a shock. It seemed remarkable that so piercing a sound could issue from so small an animal. Only rabbits can scream louder.

Eventually the horsemen gathered on the far side of the devastated colony. Distance and the hard breathing of horses drowned out their crude comments and muted their laughter as they turned and rode off together toward the upper end of the canyon. Soon the air belonged again to the song of the creek and the calling of birds, save for a flurry of anxious calls and the occasional moan.

Moving with the slowness of the damned and displaying the utter despair of those who have experienced more tragedy than is fair, the miners and their families began returning to the creek and to their homes—those that remained standing. The dust and the dirt that the invaders had stirred up didn't bother them. They lived with that every day, and a dozen horsemen raised no more soil than a good wind. It was the frequency of these malign visitations that was becoming harder and harder to bear. The frequency of them, and the certain knowledge that today's visit was not the last.

Hands recovered tools and hats from the ground and the shallow water. Men who had endured twenty-foot snows and near starvation wept silently over broken sluice boxes and bent gold pans. Those lucky ones who this time had lost but little joined together to help those less fortunate recover what they could. Somewhere an infant was crying softly, muffled and warm as its mother tried to rock it to sleep.

Near the edge of the creek Megan Wheeler knelt alongside something that resembled an old, torn shoe. She was crying silently as she picked up the tiny body. It was light in her arms, much lighter than the filled water bucket had been, and in death it appeared smaller than ever. She was choking slightly, not on her tears but on her anger, and she ignored the blood that stained her hands.

Turning, she quietly beseeched her neighbors and acquaintances for some kind of recognition of her loss, for some small expression of concern. None was forthcoming. The numbed citizens of Carbon Canyon had no sorrow to expend on a dead mongrel. They were too busy trying to reassemble their own lives from the chaos the invaders had wrought.

Megan was old enough to realize that no one could help, that there was nothing that could be done. That didn't keep her from wishing it were otherwise. She had sought sympathy and had found none. There's little sympathy in a beaten man, and the inhabitants of Carbon Canyon were just about beat. One more ride through, one more party would finish them.

Megan didn't care about that, didn't care about the future of the town-to-be or the hard-pressed people who comprised it. She cared only about the dead animal in her arms, which she had loved. She started climbing the slope toward the treeline.

Sarah saw her daughter coming and took a step in her direction, then halted. She'd been hurt deeply herself, having lost someone she'd loved, and she knew from experience that there were no simple, soothing words, no verbal tonic that could ease the pain in her daughter's heart. She knew Megan well enough to know that for now it would be better to say nothing. The girl was stubborn and determined. She would want to know *why*. She would want reasons, and Sarah had none to give. Having no answer for herself, she could not possibly have one for her grieving daughter.

So she simply stood there close by the cabin and watched as her child made her own way into the wooded upper slopes that framed the canyon. Children grew up fast in this country, and by running to Megan now Sarah knew she could do more harm than good. Then she turned her attention to the ruined laundry, the trampled vegetable garden. She had work of her own to attend to, and the sooner she started on it the less time she would have to spend thinking about it.

It was quiet in the forest. Up over the ridge and in among the pines and spruces you couldn't hear the creek, much less the resigned chatter of those eking out a living along its banks. That suited Megan just fine. She had no time for them now, not for their complaints or their excuses. Her own personal tragedy overwhelmed everything else that had happened this morning.

After a brief search she found the spot she wanted, a hollow between tree roots where falling pine needles and other debris had collected to form a thick mulch above the underlying granite. It was easy to excavate a small hole in the soft organic soil. The grave didn't have to be very big to accommodate the tiny body.

She laid the corpse of the puppy gently into the basin, then covered it with the material she'd scooped out, patting it down firmly in hopes of keeping the scavengers away for a little while, at least. It would have been better if she'd had some big rocks to put atop the grave, but there weren't any in the immediate vicinity and suddenly she was too tired to go hunting for some. The packed earth and mulch would have to suffice.

She sat back on her haunches, alone there in the silent woods, and regarded the grave. Then she recited the words she'd been taught to say at such times. But the comfort they usually gave was cold, and she couldn't keep the underlying bitterness from spreading into her voice.

"The Lord is my shepherd, I shall not want—but I *do* want. He leadeth me beside the still waters. He restoreth my soul." She paused and tilted her head back to look skyward. It was a distant sheet of cloud-flecked blue pierced by the high crowns of the tall trees that surrounded her.

"But they killed my dog! Why did you let them kill my dog?"

When no reply was forthcoming, she swallowed and forced herself to continue. "Yea, though I walk through the valley of the shadow of death, I shall fear no evil—but I'm afraid. They'll come back. I know they will. They've come before and they'll come again. Nobody talks about it. It's like if they ignore it, it'll go away, but it hasn't gone away, and it isn't going to, is it?" A longer pause this time. Might as well finish it, she told herself tiredly. For all the good it will do.

"For thou art with me. Thy rod and thy staff comfort me—but we need more than comfort. We need a miracle."

13

She licked her lips. "Mother says miracles happen, sometimes. The book says they happen. Thy loving kindness and mercy shall follow me all the days of my life—*if* you exist. And I shall dwell in the house of the Lord forever."

She rose then and stared silently down at the hidden grave. There was no need for a marker. No one else would give a damn. A few of them would laugh at her if she told them what she'd done here and asked someone to make her a cross. She didn't need one. She knew where the place was, knew she could find it again whenever she wanted. Linsey. Wasn't even growed into a proper dog yet. Didn't know enough to run like everyone else. Didn't know enough to be scared.

It was going to be lonelier than ever in the little cabin now, especially during the long winter nights to come.

Again she turned her gaze heavenward. "Understand, Lord, I *want* to dwell in your house forever, but I'd like to get a little more out of this life first, and if you don't help us, some of us are going to get hurt real bad and maybe even killed. Because those men are going to keep coming back. Please? I don't think I'm asking for too much. Just one miracle. A little one—about Linsey's size?"

She looked at the grave a last time, and wiped the tears from first the right eye, then the left. Then she turned away and started back toward the camp. Her mother would be getting worried about her. Soon she'd start searching for her, and Megan knew her mother had enough to worry about without having to concern herself with the whereabouts of a wayward daughter.

But despite her resolve to be grown-up about it, it was very difficult to leave the grove behind, and harder still to keep from looking back.

If she'd looked back maybe she might have seen the

14

horseman. Or maybe not. In order to do so she would have had to stare into the sun. It would have been hard to see him under the best of conditions. He was far away, so far it was difficult to determine whether he was resting on the near ridge or the one behind it. Both man and horse appeared tired, as if they'd ridden in from a considerable distance.

The man wore a battered mackinaw to ward off nighttime chill and a broad-brimmed hat to shield his face from the sun. Both coat and hat were tinged with the last vestiges of morning frost. Nor had he shaved recently, though whether this oversight was a matter of choice or due to a lack of congenial surroundings you couldn't tell without asking, and if given the chance you probably wouldn't ask. There was in that solemn, angular face and unwavering stare something that discouraged foolish conversation. One didn't talk to the horseman unless one had something worthwhile to say, and even then you might not be favored with a response.

He sat straight and easy in the saddle as he surveyed the world below the high ridge: the snow-covered peaks that had claimed the unfortunate Donner party back in '47; the mountain valleys running green with spruce and pine, fir and sequoia; the clear-running creeks of sweet water that filtered down out of the mountains to fill the distant American River, the river of gold.

Placer gold, easy to recover, and largely played out now, but still capable of luring with its promise men and women from around the world. Miners who followed the color back up the streams that fed the American in hopes of finding the mother lodes, the source of the yellow metal that had been discovered by accident at Sutter's Mill.

Poor old John Sutter, the horseman thought. Everyone knew the story. The gold had been discovered on his land, by

15

one of his employees. Forty-niners had run roughshod over his fields, ruining his farms and frightening off his stock. The gold had ruined his fortune and his health. The precious metal wasn't always a blessing to everyone who found it. Some people craved it, others went mad for the lack of it, a few rare souls sought to put it to good use.

As for the pale rider, he had no need of it. There were more important things to attend to. They troubled his mind this morning, and he wished he could lay them to rest.

Should be a town below, he knew, or at least a place where a tired traveler could buy a hot meal and coffee. Now *that* would be a discovery worth laying claim to. He flicked the reins of his mount just barely, but the horse understood and responded. Quadruped and biped knew and respected each other. They got along just fine. The rider didn't have to guide the animal into the autumnal forest below.

In Carbon Canyon despair gradually gave way to resignation, and resignation to work. Men dusted themselves off, physically and mentally, and started to put their lives back together. There were cabins to be repaired and, in at least one case, rebuilt. Long Toms were inspected with critical eyes. Those that were least damaged were lifted and straightened while their owners went in search of hammers and nails to repair the broken legs. Pans and picks were extricated from the water and gravel. They were more important than the sluice boxes. A sluice could be patched and repaired, but a good pick or shovel would cost a man two months' digging to replace.

The women worked their way through more domestic debris, recovering scattered utensils and personal effects while trying to make sense out of their sullied laundry. Today the evening meal would appear on the crude, knocked-together tables a few hours later than usual. Children had their uses too. According to their age they were set to work restacking firewood, washing pots and pans, and chasing temporarily liberated chickens and pigs back into sties and coops.

Not everyone was engaged in repairing the damage the riders had caused. Those who had suffered little had plenty of other work to do. At the far end of the canyon, where the stream called Carbon widened and slowed slightly, Hull Barret chucked the reins of the old buckboard and urged his mare onward. No padded lady's coach, the buckboard had been salvaged from the shell of an old Conestoga. It wasn't pretty, but it was strong enough to haul ore and provided the closest thing to public transport that existed in the canyon. At the moment, its owner was its sole passenger.

A big-boned twenty-year-old noticed its approach. The boy—for boy Eddy Conway was, a boy in the body of a man—loped down the slope where he'd been working to confront his father's friend.

"Quittin', Mr. Barret?" He glanced back up the creek. "They sure did make a mess o' things this time, didn't they?" He let out a long whistle by way of emphasis.

Hull's reply was firm. "Not quitting, Eddy. Just going into town. Somebody's got to. Some of the sluices are needin' new posts and we're running low on some other things. Nails, salt, coffee. Going to try and get some of that newfangled glue that comes in cans."

The younger Conway bestowed a guileless grin on the older man. "Ain't that awful dumb, Mr. Barret? 'Member what happened to ya last time? Ya don't want that to happen again, do ya?"

"I'll worry about it, Eddy. You get back to your work." He chucked the reins again, trying to get a little more speed out of the mare. He wanted to get clear of the canyon before any more of his friends and neighbors noticed what he was about and tried to dissuade him. He was afraid they might succeed.

Conway stepped aside. "Sure thing, Mr. Barret."

Where the creek formed a deep pool, Teddy Conway, Eddy's twin brother in body and mind, sat contently staring at the motionless tip of his fishing pole. He sat up as the wagon came trundling by:

"Quittin', Mr. Barret?"

The miner sighed. The Conway boys had hearts as big as the mountains but unfortunately not enough brains between them to tie a pair of shoes. Their daddy had to attend to the simplest domestic chores for them. To everyone's astonishment, Spider Conway managed to do just that while working his claim as well. Everyone knew that Eddy and Teddy's mother had died giving birth to them and that ever since Spider had been forced to be both mama and daddy to them. It was on account of this that the women of Carbon Canyon tolerated Spider's occasional outbursts of foul language and explosive drunkenness in their company.

At the moment, though, Hull Barret wasn't feeling very kindly or understanding towards his fellow man.

"Just going to town, Teddy," he said darkly. His tone had no effect on the youth, just as it hadn't affected his brother Eddy. Both boys were utterly innocent of the subtleties of human communication.

So he asked blithely, "Ain't that kinda dumb, Mr. Barret?"

Hull threw him a look. At least Teddy didn't say anything about what had happened the last time. The painful reminder was unnecessary. There was nothing wrong with Barret's own memory.

18

In essence, of course, the boys were right. It was stupid of him to be going to town, especially now, in light of what had happened today. But damn it, *somebody* had to go into town for supplies. Otherwise they might as well all pack up and pack it in. But as he'd just told both boys, he wasn't quittin'.

He could feel the boy's eyes on his back as he edged the buckboard around a big rock.

The blouse was worse than dirty. Flying hooves had torn one of the sleeves. Sarah's lips tightened as she retrieved it from the mud and held it up to the light. Yes, it could be patched. A shawl would hide the scar, and she could do most of the sewing under the arm, where it wouldn't show. She added it to the soiled basketful of clothing tucked under her arm. Of the widely scattered laundry, only the blouse had suffered damage. Dirt and mud could be removed. All it amounted to was a little extra work. It could have been much worse.

She started back into the cabin and just did espy the buckboard passing below.

"Hull? Hull, is that you?"

The buckboard's occupant heard the call but did not turn. He continued to stare grimly straight ahead. Sarah Wheeler was not so easily ignored, however. She put the basket aside, abandoning the laboriously recovered laundry to the wind and the elements. Picking up her hem, she raced down the slope.

"Hull Barret, you stop that wagon! I know you can hear me, Hull. You stop this instant!"

She was alongside the slowly moving wagon in a moment, panting hard as she paced it and staring up at its stony-faced driver. "Hull, you're not going into town. I won't let you."

A slight smile creased the miner's face. His reply was gentle. "'Preciate your concern, Sarah."

19

"It's more than concern; it's plain common sense. You know what I'm talking about, Hull."

He nodded tersely. "Eddy and Teddy just reminded me. Don't you start in on me too, Sarah."

"Hull, you can't go into town, Lahood's men will be there!"

"Somebody's got to do something."

"But why *you*?" She strode alongside the wagon, trying to keep her eyes on the man atop the bench seat while negotiating the uncertain footing ahead.

"Guess I'm the only fool who's determined to stick it out no matter what, Sarah," he replied quietly. "Looks like everyone else is ready to quit. Near enough, anyways. If I don't go fetch what we need, then it'll be more'n near enough. Everyone'll be gone by morning."

Then let them leave!" she snapped angrily. "They're right. We should all quit. Give Lahood what he wants. He's going to get it eventually. This patch of mud's not worth your getting hurt again. Don't you see that?"

"Guess not. Maybe it's because this patch of mud's all we got. Never had no land of my own before this. Always worked somebody else's land or somebody else's store or somebody else's farm." He jerked his head back in the direction of the settlement. "Same's true for most of the others. That's why they're here." He smiled reassuringly down at her. "Lahood's just bruised us, Sarah. He hasn't broken us. Not me, anyways."

"It'll come to that," she shot back evenly. "I swear, Hull Barret, if anything happens to you in town, I'll never speak to you again!" She tripped, caught her balance, and kicked angrily at the uneven ground as she fell behind the buckboard.

Hull sighed and pulled in on the reins. The wagon coasted

to a stop, and he waited for her to catch back up to him. This time his smile was familiar, if not proprietary.

"That's a pretty strong promise for someone who hasn't agreed to marry a man yet."

She tried to summon up an appropriate reply, only to find she had nothing to say. Barret's point was well made and it was one she couldn't easily refute. She backed away from the buckboard and lowered her eyes.

Hull pushed his hat back on his forehead. "Anything you want from the store 'long as I'm gonna be there?"

Her reply was subdued. "No. Megan and I are okay." She looked up at him again, an entirely different expression on her face, pleading for understanding as much with her eyes as with her words. "It's not that I don't appreciate all you've done for Megan and me, Hull. It isn't that at all. I just—"

"Appreciation's a fine thing," he said, interrupting her. "It just never did much to keep a man warm through a long winter's night, is all." He stared back at her for a long moment. When it became evident she wasn't going to respond, he shrugged imperceptibly and flicked the reins. The wagon resumed its downhill course, leaving Sarah Wheeler standing by herself next to the creek, weighed down with the burden of her own indecision.

It wasn't right. It wasn't fair for him to challenge her like that, to make her feel the way she was feeling. It was still too soon, and she was still too bitter about what had happened to her before Hull Barret. There wasn't anything she could do about that. He was just going to have to understand, and if he couldn't, well, that was too bad for him.

But she couldn't bear to go back up to the cabin until his buckboard had vanished from sight.

II

At eight years of age, the boy Ebenezer was more than old enough to be aware of the difference between right and wrong, just as he was old enough to understand the concept of stealing. So he knew precisely what he was doing while he waited for Ma Blankenship to turn away from the counter. Two of the many glass candy jars were standing open, and he'd long since made his selection.

Now he reached quickly into the nearest, seizing the largest of the candy canes stored within, and shoved it into the pocket of his velvet coat. Seeing that the old woman was still occupied with something below the counter, he headed for the entrance, intending to make good his escape.

Since his attention was focused on the busy proprietress he didn't see the shape that was blocking his exit until he ran into it. It was hard and unyielding. His eight-year-old body bounced off, only to have a steady hand grab him to prevent him from falling.

He blinked and looked up into the strangest eyes he'd ever made contact with. Most adults, Ebenezer had discovered, did not look at children. They looked around them, or through them, or at their clothing or hair, but never into their eyes. Not this man. Big as he was, he was staring straight back at Ebenezer. It was a new sensation, and not altogether a comfortable one.

One thing Ebenezer was certain of: this stranger had been there long enough to have witnessed the theft of the candy cane. But in that case, why hadn't he said something by now?

22

Ebenezer risked a fearful glance in Ma Blankenship's direction, but she was still busy behind the counter. She wasn't eyeing him accusingly in response to some secret adult look from the stranger.

Still the man said nothing. Was it possible he *hadn't* seen? It seemed impossible. Ebenezer held onto his look of defiance a moment longer, but he was badly overmatched. It was kind of like trying to outstare the family cat, which wouldn't put up for long with such nonsense from Ebenezer or any of his siblings. Somehow he knew that this stranger's patience wouldn't last much longer either.

Guiltily he reached into his picket and brought out one of the several pennies that resided therein. The stranger let him go. He walked back to the counter, put the penny next to the open candy jar, and then hastened out the doorway. The stranger followed him with his eyes and with just the slightest of smiles.

Then he turned back to survey the interior of the general store. Considering the size of the town it was well stocked and prosperous looking. That made it unusual, but not unique. California was starting to fill up with men and women who were smart enough to realize that the best way to get their hands on some gold was to let others do the digging for them. There was gold in the ground and there was gold in bolts of calico and sacks of sugar for sale, too.

Off to the left stood a trestle counter populated by a brace of hand-hewn stools. Keeping his mackinaw buttoned, the tall man sat down on one stool that looked a little sturdier than the others. He was conscious of his size and always had care for someone else's furniture. He was six foot four and broad in proportion, and the petite chairs often favored by store owners for their female customers sometimes displayed the disconcerting habit of collapsing beneath him, to the chagrin of both the proprietor and his visitor. But these stools had been fashioned by men who also built railroad trestles and sluice boxes and mine carts. The one he'd chosen did not creak beneath him when he placed his full weight upon it.

He was much harder to overlook than the boy who'd just fled the store. The woman who had been working at the cutting board behind the counter turned to greet him. As she spoke she toweled fresh bread dough from her hands. Fiftyish, matronly in appearance and pleasant of voice and countenance, she gave the stranger the impression that she could deal on an equal basis with tough miners or the wives of the wealthy.

"Mornin', stranger. I'm Carlotta Blankenship, but everybody hereabouts calls me Ma. You might as well too, and I don't think your own ma would mind. Welcome to Lahood, California." She gestured expansively. "Only place on Earth they cut the seasons down to three: winter, July, and August. What'll you have?"

"Just coffee, thanks."

Her eyes narrowed slightly and she regarded her customer with fresh curiosity. Odd sort of voice. Came from the back of the throat and not the lips or mouth. Sort of whispered out at you. It reminded her of something, and it took her a second to remember.

A steam radiator. She'd once stayed in a room in San Francisco that had been heated by such a device. That was just what this tall visitor sounded like when he spoke.

"Pardon me for sayin' so, but you look like you could use something a mite solider." She nodded back toward the cutting board where she'd been working. "Have some fresh bread ready in a while. Supposed to save the first loaves for the Cutter boys, but they'll likely be late as usual. So if you'd like some . . . '' She let the offer trail off meaningfully. "Got some fresh blackberry jam, too.''

His initial reply came in the form of a winning, almost boyish smile. "Sounds good. Coffee first, then maybe I'll work up to the other. If I have enough time.''

Lahood, California, was a far cry from Sacramento or San Francisco. The town was composed of no more than half a dozen permanent buildings flanking a muddy main street. Tents and lean-tos clustered around the town's outskirts. Their owners aspired to wood and plaster but found better uses for their gold.

The foothills of the Sierra Nevada encroached on the east side of the community, smooth, rolling, and deceptively modest in size. Shrouded in mist, beyond rose the first of the granite ramparts that formed the Range of Light. These were covered in snow and ice the year 'round.

Not everyone living in California was engaged in the mad hunt for gold that year. Someone had to provide the miners with tools and victuals. Someone had to bury the unlucky, someone had to cut hair, and someone had to assist with births as more and more women followed gold hungry men into the new state. They filled up the burgeoning cities and trickled out into new towns like Placerville and Bad Flats and Lahood.

Some strolled along the duckboard planks that enabled ladies to keep their feet out of the mud while others worked to load a freighting dray outside the big feed store. A few horsemen trotted down the main street, eyeing the sky and wondering if this winter would be as hard as the last.

From the northern end of town a buckboard could be seen as it approached, its single horse plodding townward slowly and patiently.

The barber-cum-dentist was busily engaged in extracting a broken tooth from the mouth of a customer with all the skill and delicacy of touch that his patient would use to blast quartz matrix from the surrounding granite. Both dentist and patient strained mightily. A powerful yank on the iron pliers and the rotten molar emerged, along with a barely stifled grunt of pain from its stoic former owner.

Tossing the tooth into a nearby metal pail, the dentist paused long enough to glance streetward. He did not expect to see anything of unusual note. This was Lahood, after all. So he was doubly surprised to see the buckboard as it rolled past his establishment.

"I'll be damned," he muttered, moving toward the window for a better look.

His pain momentarily forgotten, the patient sat up in his chair and let his eyes follow the dentist's gaze. "What, what is it?"

"Barret."

Holding his aching jaw with one hand, the miner pushed aside the sheet that had been used to cover him and joined the dentist in gaping out the window.

"Danged if it ain't," he breathed in amazement.

In the newly built United States Post Office the tight-lipped postmistress was taking letters from a sheaf held firmly in one hand and placing them in their respective pigeonholes on the wall oposite. A chance look in the direction of the multipaned windows revealed the buckboard wending its way down the main street. She paused, one letter halfway to its destination, to stare at the driver.

So did the undertaker, who left off painting a newly fashioned pine casket to observe the passing wagon in silence. When he resumed his work he was whistling softly.

26

California in the midfifties was full of business for a man in his profession. He'd done right well there in little Lahood, though some of the business that was brought his way required the utmost skill and patience his art could muster. Very few of his clients died a natural death. Some of them had met their demise in noisy and spectacular fashion. It wasn't always an easy task to make them presentable for the last time. A post-Gold Rush mortician tended to earn his money.

Unaware that he was the object of so much attention, Hull Barret guided the buckboard down the right side of the street, where the mud was shallower. His head never wavered, but his eyes were in constant motion, darting from right to left and back again. He examined each building in turn as he passed it, paying particular attention to each door and half-opened window.

It was with considerable relief that he reined in the mare and tied her up to the hitching rail outside his destination. It was an imposing structure. A large sign both identified it and proclaimed ownership.

BLANKENSHIP MERCANTILE

A lone gelding was the only other animal tied up outside, a fact that Hull noted with additional relief. As he worked at securing the reins he couldn't keep his gaze from straying to the building directly across the street. It was even more impressive than Blankenship's emporium. The two-story office and warehouse was surmounted by a massive sign of its own, the letters bold and challenging.

C. K. LAHOOD & SON
Mining and Smelting

There were chairs on the porch that faced the street. Three of them were presently occupied by a trio of Lahood's roustabouts. One of them recognized Hull and gestured. The three exchanged whispers and even across the street Hull could make out their faint, unpleasant laughter. He doubted they were talking politics.

Nothing much to be done about it now. He was committed, and they'd seen him. What was he worrying about, anyway? He had as much right to come into town as anyone else, including Lahood's flunkies.

Sure he did.

He added a protective clove hitch to the reins, the men's distant sniggering loud in his ears. Ignoring it as best he could, he climbed the steps leading to the store. He was inordinately glad once he was inside. Not that that would make any difference if anything happened, but if felt good to have their eyes off him.

Jed Blankenship watched him enter. The owner of the general store was seated on a stool behind the hardware counter. He looked his sixty years, and wore shirtsleeve garters and an accountant's visor as well as the attitude of a man who at that moment would rather have been someplace else. Ordinarily he was delighted to greet his customers, that they might enrich his coffers, but he was not pleased to see Hull Barret enter. He leaned slightly to his right to peer out the open door. The street was empty. For the moment.

Ah well. Blankenship was both kindly and Christian. He was also hard as nails. He could always abandon his seat and make a dash for the back room if trouble broke out. Actually he was more upset by Barret's timing than by his presence.

"Damn fool," he muttered to himself. "Couldn't you have waited 'til the smoke cleared away?"

"Afternoon, Mr. B." Hull's voice was full of forced cheerfulness. "We seem to be in need of a few supplies."

Blankenship responded with a grunt. "Whole new camp, the way I hear it." He shook his head and looked at his visitor reprovingly. "You got sand, boy, but you ain't got the sense God gave a sack o' beans. You need something, that's for sure, and it ain't supplies. Couldn't you have at least waited a day or two before coming in?"

"Didn't have much choice. They ruined the MacPherson shack, damaged a couple others. Got to fix 'em now, before the weather starts to set in. If it rained, some kids up there could catch their deaths. We wouldn't want that to happen, now would we? Then there's a bunch of sluices down. They're in want of nails and some brads."

Affecting an air of nonchalance which he didn't feel, Hull started gathering up the supplies he'd come in for: a big roll of tarry construction paper, a bucket of big nails, a small keg of pitch. His eyes passed beyond the hardware department and over into the clothing. He could sure use another pair of Mr. Strauss's work pants, and there was a hat there that would look just right sitting atop a certain lady's head. But he could afford those only with a look, and that was not legal tender in Blankenship's emporium.

The proprietor's gaze narrowed as he watched the pile grow larger. "I expect you're going to pay for all this in gold, right? All that gold you've been working so hard to dig out of that damn canyon? All the gold you keep telling everyone is up there, just under the upper layer of gravel?"

"Yup," Hull replied easily. "Soon as we put together a couple ounces, I'll bring 'em in."

Blankenship pursed his lips and pulled a hardbacked ledger from the shelf behind him, drawing it forth with the speed and skill of a gunfighter drawing effortlessly on his opponent. He laid the ledger flat on the counter in front of him, opened it, and began flipping through the tall pages until he came to the one he wanted.

"It'll take a damnsite more'n a couple of ounces, Hull. Last payment of any kind that you folks made was—let's see." He flipped a page and ran a finger down an unseen column. "Eight months ago, when old Lindquist brought in a small bag of dust." He looked sharply up at his visitor, regarding him narrowly. The bridge of the visor he wore shaded his eyes but did nothing to soften his stare.

"Ever occur to any of you people there ain't no gold left in Carbon Creek? Not every river in the Sierra's full of gold, you know. Might be you folks lit on a poor one."

"If that's so, then why's Lahood so set on drivin' us out? That man never did anything didn't have money behind it. 'Course, I suppose he could just be plain cussed mean. Probably is, but if that's all that was settin' him to harassin' us, I'd think he'd of got his satisfaction by now."

"Might be," Blankenship allowed. "But one thing's sure: he means to have that canyon to himself, whether there's any gold in it or not. Maybe he ain't doing it for any gold. Maybe it's the principle of the thing to him. Might be he wants it just 'cause you folks are saying no to him."

"Might be, Mr. B., except for one thing."

"What might that be?"

"We all know Coy Lahood ain't got no principles. Anyways, you're wrong about the gold. There's color in the creek and plenty of it. You've had some of it yourself, in payment for goods received."

Blankenship let out a derisive snort. "Dust! Color! Every sourdough in California finds color."

"Not just color then. Nuggets, too. Spider panned one out this morning that was big as your fingernail. You don't find nuggets like that in played-out streams."

That made Blankenship sit up and take notice. "Spider Conway?"

Hull nodded. "The same."

Again the gunfighter glanced downward. "Found a nugget big as a fingernail, did he? Well then when you get back you tell that son-of-a-bitch I've got him down for eighty-five dollars and thirty-three cents. That's just what he owes me. I can't even imagine what he owes you and the others by now, for picking up supplies for him and those two idiot boys of his."

Hull selected a small bottle from a rack filled with narrow-mouthed containers and added it to the growing pile. "*Forty*-three cents. He wanted some arsenic to bleach his dust."

"That tears it!" The storeowner rose from his seat and jabbed a warning finger in Hull's direction. "I'm a Christian man and I do my best to be understanding, but every man's got his limit and by thunder, I've reached mine! You tell Spider and the rest of 'em that this is the end of the line. The teat's gone dry. No more credit, y'hear? No more until you pay up on what you all owe me. Hull, are you listening to me?"

By way of reply Hull grinned at him while casually adding a roll of oilcloth, two small panes of glass, and several two-by-fours to the pile that was accumulating in the middle of the floor. Lifting as much as he could carry safely in one trip, he started for the door.

"You're a decent man, Mr. B. That's why we've always brought you our trade. You know that I, that we all appreciate—"

31

Blankenship cut him off. "Don't try coddling me with words, son. Words ain't fit for much and payin' bills certainly ain't one of 'em." But the merchant's rage had already abated, just as Hull knew it would. Slowly he sat back down on his stool.

"I ain't doin' this for you," he muttered. "Hell, I'm the only merchant in town that Lahood doesn't own. Oh, most of 'em have got their own names out on their shingles, but we all know which piper they pay so's they can stay in business. It does my soul good to see a few other horns in his hide."

"Besides which maybe bein' so busy with us keeps him from figurin' out how to buy you out?" Hull ventured.

"That'll be the day!" Blankenship wagged that finger at his customer a second time. "But I'm serious this go-round, Hull. I can't afford to keep carrying you folks forever."

"We know that, Mr. B." Hull paused in the doorway long enough to look back at his aggrieved benefactor. "One day we'll hit it big up there, you'll see, and when that happens I'll pay you off in full myself. With interest." He nudged the double doors wider to make room for his load.

"Barret." Hull turned a last time. "You get your goods in the wagon and skedaddle. Just keep moving, no matter what they say." He nodded significantly toward the window and the unkempt trio lounging outside the Lahood building.

Hull nodded briskly, then made his way through the portal. Blankenship followed his progress anxiously. Damn fool, he murmured to himself. Good man but a damn fool.

Ma Blankenship craned her neck, trying to watch the street outside while simultaneously tending to her kitchen. Her thoughts as she watched Hull Barret load the wagon were similar to her husband's, though she viewed the miner in a more charitable light.

As for the single stranger she was serving, there was no telling what he thought of the minor drama that had just transpired. He sat quietly and sipped at his coffee.

Hull dumped the supplies in the back of the buckboard rather more hastily than he intended and hurried back inside for the rest. The last double armload contained Conway's arsenic as well as a small but precious vial of mercury. He put the two bottles in his pocket, then arranged the load as best he could before he began to tie down the tarp over the pile.

Across the street the three men exchanged a silent glance. Then they rose, one on the heels of the next, and started to saunter over toward the buckboard. Noting their approach, Hull tried to work twice as fast without appearing to. He didn't make a very good job of hiding his concern, and this served to amuse the three who spread out to confront him.

Their leader was one of Lahood's foremen. Hull recognized him immediately; a not too bright but thoroughly nasty bastard name of McGill. The foreman was a useful animal of the sort that Lahood was fond of employing. He was also just intelligent enough to be amused by his own wit.

"We got a beef with you, Barret."

Hull finished securing the supplies, then deliberately walked over to the hitching rail to untie his horse. This gave him a chance to identify the foreman's companions, a pair of mean-tempered gully-whompers named Jagou and Tyson. Innocent souls compared to the foreman, but just as capable of causing trouble if they thought they could get away with it.

McGill knew the miner recognized them. That was the idea. They had neither the need nor the desire to keep their identities a secret. It was important that Barret know that.

They closed in around the miner, the other two seemingly oblivious to his presence. They didn't appear in the least interested in what Hull might do, secure as they were in the knowledge that he could do nothing. McGill stepped between the miner and the wagon.

"You know, you ain't very polite, Barret. When we rode through the canyon this morning you plumb forgot to say hello." Tyson let out an evil snigger while Jagou just smiled, showing bent and broken teeth.

"We told you to stay out of town a while back, seems to me," the smiler told him, awash in fake amiability.

"Yeah, you ain't got much of a memory." Tyson grinned as he kicked at the dirt. "I remember that clear as day." He cast a doleful eye on the foreman. "Last time he come through, 'stay outta town,' you said. Then you kicked him in the head. Must've popped his memory."

"Or somethin' like that," McGill agreed.

Jagou looked thoughtful. "Maybe if we kicked him again, it'd all come back to him."

Hull stepped past McGill and mounted the buckboard, taking up the reins. If the wagon had been positioned differently, he would've taken a chance by whipping the reins, but with it pointing towards the store instead of the street and with the hitching rail and watering trough directly in front of him there was no way he could move in a hurry. Damn. He should have thought of that when he'd pulled in. Too late for it now.

McGill moved around to one side of the wagon while Tyson and Jagou remained on the other, grinning up at the miner.

"You ain't real talkative today, are you, Barret?" McGill feigned disappointment. "What's wrong? Nothing new up in the canyon? I thought after this morning you'd have plenty to talk about. Don't you want to tell us about how you're doin' up there?''

"Yeah, how about them Wheeler women?" Jagou leered up at him. "You hump the growed one, or you hump 'em both?"

Hull's fingers tightened on the reins until they whitened and the tendons in his neck went taut. Delighted at having hooked his fish on the first cast, Jagou continued to play the line.

"That little one's just out o' knickers, ain't she?" He chuckled. "Bet she's juicy as a freshwater clam, huh?" He leaned close, his eyes bright, broken teeth gleaming. "C'mon, Barret, you kin tell us. Don't you want to share with your friends? Why, we might want to get us a little some time, and I'd be grateful for some pointers."

"Yeah, Barret." Tyson rushed to join in. "Tell us: when you hump 'em, you have the little one on top or on the bottom?"

Somehow Hull kept control of himself, seated on the narrow seat, his back rigid and his hands trembling. McGill pushed back his hat and stood surveying the miner in disbelief.

"You just beat all, Barret. What's it take to get you down off that seat and fight like a man? We have to bust your goods again?" He gestured toward the back of the wagon and the stack of irreplaceable supplies.

Hull's lips parted. Words emerged, easy with enforced calm. "I didn't come here to fight."

McGill nodded disgustedly, looking as though he'd been anticipating such a reply. "That's what wrong with you. You and the rest o' them tin-pan squatters. You ain't got no balls, none of you." Turning, he walked around to the rear of the wagon and flipped up the unsecured back edge of the tarpaulin.

Hull whirled. "Leave 'em be!"

A broad smile creased McGill's face. "Well now, what about this? Seems as how you can talk when you've a mind to, though I don't think much of a man who worries more about his supplies than his women." He studied the pile. "Don't see why you're so damn concerned about this junk anyways. Not much here but tarpaper and wood. Good makin's for a fire, though. Right, boys?"

"Oh yeah, a fire," said Tyson quickly.

Jagou rubbed his hands together in expectation. "Sure is, boss. It is a mite cold out today."

McGill reached into a pocket and brought out a match, then struck it alight on the side of the buckboard. He spoke as it flared to life, watching as it burned down toward his fingers.

"Better get down from that seat now, Barret. It might get hot all of a sudden, though if what I hear tell about them Wheeler women is half right, you're probably used to that by now."

So saying, he flipped the match onto the oilcloth. Hull was out of his seat instantly, flailing at the incipient bonfire with the unfastened edge of the tarp. He just managed to extinguish the flames before McGill grabbed his ankles and yanked hard.

Overbalanced on the back of the wagon and without anything to brace himself against, Hull struck the side of the buckboard and fell over into the street. The three men were on top of him before he could regain his footing. The flat sound of fists striking flesh seemed preternaturally loud in the clear mountain air.

No one saw the hand that silently removed the big oak bucket from its hook next to the watering trough. It was dipped into the icy water and the contents then dumped onto the back of the wagon. There was more than enough in the single bucketful to douse the smouldering remnant of the fire.

The bucket was a solid, no-nonsense piece of work. It made a loud *crack* when it slammed down against the back of Jagou's neck. The roustabout went down as if he'd been poleaxed and his two companions looked up in shock. They barely had enough time to register their surprise before the bucket descended a second time. It smashed Tyson's hat flat against his skull. He fell over on top of the unconscious Jagou.

McGill raised a hand to ward off the coming blow, and the bucket splintered against his jaw, sending him sprawling in the mud.

It was all over in less than a minute.

Jagou lay on his belly while Tyson started rolling and moaning, clutching at his skull. McGill slowly worked his jaw, which miraculously had remained in place. None of the three had any thoughts of fighting back.

Ignoring them and whatever they might choose to do, the stranger lifted the remains of the bucket and eyed it critically. There wasn't much left except the wire handle.

"Don't make 'em like they used to," he murmured to no one in particular.

Hanging the wire strap back on its hook, he bent and got both arms under Hull Barret's, lifting the stunned miner to his feet. Hull said nothing as the stranger helped him remount the buckboard. This done, his mysterious benefactor then mounted the gelding tied up nearby, turned, and gave Hull's animal a whack on its rump. The buckboard lurched forward, then to the side as the stranger guided it out to the middle of the street. Together they rode toward the far end of town.

Hull had completely forgotten his own injuries. The tall man riding alongside the wagon appeared none the worse for wear. He didn't look back and he wasn't so much as breathing hard. But Hull looked back. He had to. It was the only sure way he had of convincing himself he hadn't dreamed the last five minutes.

He could see a shaky McGill standing over his cronies, who were still down in the dirt. They were in no condition to walk across the street, much less mount any kind of vengeful pursuit. Thus reassured, he removed his bandana from a pocket and began wiping at the blood that covered his face.

He tried to see everything a second time in his mind. Everything was fairly clear up to the point when the stranger had intervened. Then a brief blur of action, the bucket whizzing through the air like a medieval mace, and suddenly he was back on the buckboard instead of lying there in the street having the beejeesus knocked out of him.

It was all pretty hazy, but he was certain of one thing: the stranger had done it alone, without any help from anyone on the street or inside the store. One man had done what the whole town wouldn't have dared.

He gazed at his benefactor with a mixture of gratitude and unadulterated awe, but all he could think of to say was, "Obliged."

The tall rider's smile came quick and easy. It made you want to smile back.

"Those men hold some kind of grudge against you? Three against one's not fair odds."

Depends on who the one is, Hull thought admiringly. "Would've stayed out of it if they'd have let me." He wiped at the bridge of his nose and winced. Sore but not broken. He had reason to be thankful for that. Lahood was not big enough to afford a full-time physician and the barber-dentist didn't count.

"Tried to. Didn't work any better this time than the last. It's a bit more'n a grudge. Feud's more like it. Some folks would call it business, I guess. My name's Barret. Hull Barret."

The stranger simply nodded by way of reply. Nodded and smiled. Friendly enough, and more than helpful, Hull decided as he regarded his companion, but not overly informative. Well, that was okay with Hull. You didn't push a man in such matters, not in gold country. Most men had come to California seeking the yellow metal, but not a few had come in search of anonymity. Yes, that was fine with Hull. Anything the tall stranger might choose to do was fine with him.

It did nothing to sate his curiosity, though, and he couldn't resist asking, "You from hereabouts?"

"Nope."

My, but he was talkative. "Placerville? he asked, forgetting his own advice to himself. "Sacramento maybe?"

A single shake of head and hat. "Uh-uh."

Hull Barret hadn't stuck it out on Carbon Creek for this long because of a lack of persistence. So long as the man gave no indication of taking offense, the miner felt it would be all right to continue with his inquiries.

"Just passing through, then."

The stranger shrugged indifferently. "Maybe. Maybe not. Guess I hadn't given it a whole lot of thought."

Interesting, Hull mused. Interesting and maybe, just maybe, useful. He tried not to sound too anxious. "After what you did back there, I wouldn't stay in town if I was you. You stuck your foot in a hornet's nest. I wouldn't advise sleeping nearby. My cabin's got two rooms." He nodded toward the mountains looming just ahead. "It's not the Palace, but it keeps out the wind and most of the rain, and the beds ain't under the leaks. You're welcome to one of 'em for as long as you'd like to stay."

The stranger mulled this offer over before replying. "Thanks. That's kind of you, but I wouldn't want to be a burden on your family."

It was Hull's turn to smile. "My family's back east, dead and buried. Got a fiancée, is all. But she and her daughter have a place of their own. So I've got plenty of room. It'd be a pleasure to me if you'd stay, not a burden. I'd enjoy the company, and we don't get to see too may new faces in Carbon. Give me somebody new to jaw at, somebody who ain't heard all my old jokes, and I'm plumb delighted."

"I don't know . . ."

"You got business elsewhere?" Hull's heart began to sink.

"Not especially."

"Well then come on. Three hots and a cot's the least I owe you."

The stranger appeared to think on it further. Or maybe he'd already make his decision and was thinking about something else entirely. Hull couldn't tell. He considered himself a decent appraiser of both men and ore, but this quiet stranger was an enigma to him.

A reply, at last. "Sounds good."

Pleased with himself, Hull straightened on the hard seat. Ignoring the pain this caused him (McGill had spent a moment or two on his back and the result was slow in disappearing), he chucked the reins to urge the mare to greater speed. Having received a commitment, he didn't want to give the stranger a chance to change his mind.

Gradually the road disappeared. A trail veered northward,

and Hull turned the wagon onto the barely visible track that led up into the mountains. Low scrub gave way to tall evergreens and rolling foothills made room for steep granite walls with breathtaking speed. The metamorphosis never failed to amaze the Easterner in Hull Barret. These were not civilized mountains like the Adirondacks or the Alleghenies. One minute you were on the outskirts of the great central valley and the next, you were traveling through a granite cathedral.

He tried to make conversation with his companion, putting aside personal questions in favor of sallies on the weather, the cost of goods, and of course, the possible sources and locations of gold. When it became clear that his pleasant but nearly mute friend wasn't interested in talk, the miner shut up. Maybe the tall rider was tired, or maybe he was thinking about the consequences of his actions back there in town. Hull didn't think that was the case, but he had the feeling that with this man you couldn't be sure of much of anything.

They rode on in contemplative silence, Barret's mind churning furiously with hopes and plans, the other rider apparently content to absorb the beauty of the scenery. It took most of what remained of the day for them to reach the diggings.

III

He didn't say much, but Hull suspected his companion missed nothing as they rode into Carbon Canyon. Not that there was much to see. There were ten thousand canyons just like it that cut into the western flank of the Sierra Nevada. Surely he'd seen copies of Carbon elsewhere. But he looked interested all the same.

Hull pointed up the slope. "That's my place, there. Just draw a straight line from that damned boulder that marks the middle of my claim. One of these days I'm going to—but we can talk about that later, if we have the time. I'm sure you ain't in the mood for chitchat now. I don't know how long you've been riding, but you must be tuckered out right proper after that scrape back in town."

The stranger spoke without looking over at him, apparently intent on committing the surrounding terrain to memory. "I've been on the trail awhile."

Somehow Hull restrained himself from asking "How long?" and "Where from?" "You'll find water and shaving gear inside. I'll tell Sarah—that's my fiancée—there'll be an extra mouth to feed, and I need to share out these supplies I picked up before dark." He chuckled. "Bet there's some folks who didn't think they'd ever see 'em. Got you to thank for that. Won't take long. Just make yourself at home."

There was more he wanted to say, much more he wanted to tell his new companion. It would have to wait. Ordinarily Hull Barret wasn't much of a talker, but since this stranger was proving to be such a good listener he felt the words flowing freely. There was something about the tall rider that inspired confidence, and it was more than just his recently demonstrated physical prowess.

He didn't get the chance in any case, because they were confronted by an older man leading a heavily laden mule downstream. He was half blond and half gray, and he looked older than his years. He met Barret's inquisitive stare unashamedly.

"So long, Hull."

"Where you going, Ulrik?" Hull frowned, glanced skyward. "Kind of late to be going into town."

"I bane not goin' into that damned town. I yust goin'. Gettin' out while I still can."

Hull pulled back on the reins, bringing the wagon to a halt. The old Swede led his mule around the obstacle. "Gettin' out?" Hull repeated. "Where the hell to?"

"Don't matter. Someplace where I bane not goin' get ruined day after day. Some place where I can sleep nights. Can't fight no more, Hull. I bane not the only one, neither."

Hull had to turn to look back at the departing miner. "Aw, Ulrik. You know what they say. 'It's bound to get better 'cause it can't get any worse.'"

The old man nodded knowingly. "Man that said that hain't been livin' in Carbon Canyon. Goodbye and good luck, Hull Barret. You'll quit too, if you're smart."

Hull watched until man and mule had passed beyond earshot. Shaking his head in silent disappointment, he turned forward again and urged the mare onward.

"What was that all about?" the stranger inquired mildly.

The other man's expression was set, his voice low. "Remember that feud I told you about? Ulrik's leavin' has to do with it. I'll explain later. Doesn't concern you in any case." So saying, he risked a quick glance in the stranger's direction. If he was expecting a follow-up query or an expression of more than casual interest, he was disappointed. The tall rider was staring straight ahead, apparently having accepted Hull's declaration at face value.

Hull shrugged. He had supplies to distribute and he wanted to be done with that before dark.

The stranger surveyed the cabin. Two separate rooms, as its owner had claimed. Facilities out back. But it was clean and neat and in much better condition than the average miner's abode. This was no knocked-together lean-to meant to be abandoned each winter. It was a permanent, year-round dwelling, put together with care and expertise and not a few hard-won dollars. There was glass in the windows and linen on the beds. Hull Barret took pride in his little cabin, and it showed.

Just as it showed in the man, the stranger mused to himself.

He moved into the back room and set out his kit, paid a quick visit to the one-holer out back, then returned and considered what to do next. Hull was right about him having ridden a long ways, and he was more than a little tired, but there were going to be ladies at supper. He rubbed at the thick stubble that covered his face. Proper thing to do was to clean up some.

In the front room he found a big washbasin full of water that had been allowed to sit in a south-facing window all day. As a result, the water in both the basin and its accompanying pitcher was almost hot. A brief search turned up soap and a razor. The soap was not homemade lye, as he expected. It was bar soap and it smelled of lilac. Imported by someone like Blankenship all the way from San Francisco, no doubt. He eyed the precious bar approvingly. Blankenship wouldn't sell luxury goods on credit. There had to be some gold in this canyon, then.

He stripped off his mackinaw and shirt, then pulled the undershirt over his head and laid it out neatly on the nearby cot. There were no noticeable scars on his chest, but the ones on his back would have caught the eye of the most indifferent observer. There were five of them. Each was a half inch in diameter and evenly spaced from its neighbor. They formed a neat circle. Though long since healed over, their origin was unmistakeable.

They were bullet holes.

Evening sunlight poured through the window above the washbasin, illuminating the stranger's face as he gazed at himself in the unframed mirror and plied the razor with long, sure strokes, removing lather and whiskers. The unmuted light highlighted the angles and planes of his face, throwing unsuspected ravines and depressions into sharp relief. Once shorn of its whiskers, it was a face whose topography most closely resembled that of the rugged mountains that comprised the Sierra crest.

A voice made him pause. The voice came from outside and was unmistakably feminine. Turning from the mirror, be bent to squint out the window, finding a clear space between the bubbles in the cheap glass. Two women, moving past Hull's cabin toward another. His fiancée and her daughter, he decided. They were hauling a black iron kettle between them, unaware they were being watched.

The stranger allowed his gaze to linger briefly on the two figures until they disappeared into another shanty nearby. They had looked so out of place amidst this harsh wilderness of tree and rock. By their very presence they helped to soften and civilize it. If he didn't get a move on, he told himself, he'd be late.

He turned back to the mirror and prepared to finish shaving. What he saw made him hesitate, the razor hovering an inch from his neck. There was something in the eyes that stared back at him, something distant and sad, and a touch of longing for something lost long ago. There was one other thing, more immediate and not nearly as pleasant.

He'd look mighty funny showing up at the table with his face half shaved, he decided. The razor moved.

Megan arranged the forks and plates just so around the edge of the split-board table. Then she stepped back to examine her handiwork with a critical eye. Evidently dissatisfied, she rearranged the entire table setting for the third time.

Her mother was hard at work at the big cast-iron woodstove behind the table, stirring the simmering contents of the big kettle with a heavy wooden spoon. From time to time she glanced to her right, but the door to the back room remained closed.

It would've been much easier to have served supper in their own cabin, but Hull insisted the food be moved to his own, the better to accommodate his "guest." She worked the spoon around the inside of the kettle, trying hard to hold her temper. Guest indeed! But there was no swaying Hull. A good man, Hull Barret, but with no taste in companions. Still, having agreed to this supper, there was little she could do now except go through with it.

Hull was pacing back and forth between table and stove, unable to keep from talking but keeping his voice low.

"It was the damndest thing you ever saw, Sarah. There I was, lying on the ground with those three SOB's of Lahood's on top of me, and suddenly they're not there anymore. One two three bam! Just like that, they're gone. Then I see that they're rolling around in the mud hollerin' and moanin', and this big guy's just standing there over 'em real quiet like, lookin' like he's bored with the whole thing." He shook his head at the remembrance.

"The way he waded into McGill and his men, you should've seen him. I was kind of groggy at the time, but I could see he wasn't even breathing hard. He might as well have been smashing roaches out back."

Sarah kept her attention and her gaze on the steaming kettle. So far she had steadfastly refused to share in Hull's misplaced enthusiasm.

"He sounds no different from McGill or Tyson, or any of Lahood's roughnecks." Lifting the kettle off the iron, she set it on the table and began ladling stew into bowls.

Hull halted. "At least he wasn't afraid of them. He rode on out of town with his back toward 'em, as though he couldn't care less what they might do about it. That's what we need up here. Someone they can't scare."

Finally satisfied with the table arrangements, Megan Wheeler peered thoughtfully at her mother's friend. She liked Hull Barret, though she was too shy to ever say so. He was her friend, too, and had been ever since . . .

She swallowed. "Are you scared of them, Hull? I didn't think you were scared of anything."

"He should be," Sarah snapped before he could reply, "but he's too all-fired stubborn."

"But I *was* scared. That's the point, Sarah. I ain't ashamed to admit it. There were three of 'em, and all bigger than me, and I had the supplies to worry about, too. They had me scared and they knew it. It wasn't them, though. It's Lahood who's done that to us. Got us all scared." He turned and walked over to a window to peer out at the canyon. Beautiful it was in the last light of day. A few die-hards still worked their claims but for the most part the camp was silent. Off to the left and downslope he could just make out the twang of

47

Skinny Smith's battered banjo. It was clean and peaceful, the canyon was.

If only Lahood would leave them alone.

"Something else. On my way back from town I passed Ulrik Lindquist. He was ridin' out. Had his mule with him and looked like everything else, too. He didn't even know where he was going. 'Just goin',' he said. I remember when he first came up here, he didn't talk like that. All he could talk about was how much gold he was going to pan out of the creek and how he was going to spend it in Frisco. To see him ride out like that—you should've seen his eyes, Sarah. It was plumb pitiful, and worst of it was I didn't know what to say to try and stop him."

"What could you have said?" Sarah sounded resigned. "The colony's beaten, Hull. It's everyone, not just poor Ulrik. The only one who doesn't know it is you."

"And me." Megan stared defiantly at the creek outside. "They're not driving me away. I'm not leaving until Lahood and his men are whipped. Every last one of them."

"Hush, Megan!" Sarah threw Hull an accusatory look. "See what you're doing, Hull Barret? Such language. She talks more like your daughter than mine. I didn't raise her up to go thinking such thoughts. Tell her it's nonsense, this business of fighting Lahood."

Hull tried to affect an air of innocence, but didn't succeed very well. "Who said anything about fighting?"

"You did, talking about this, this stranger." She waved the spoon in the direction of the back bedroom door. "What is he, a gunslinger? Or worse?"

Exasperated but unable to bring himself to shout back at the woman he loved, Hull found some solace in the bottle of whiskey he kept on the top kitchen shelf. It was real whiskey, brought in by train all the way from Sacramento, and it was considerably more precious and expensive than his store-bought soap. Much as he adored Sarah, he found that there were times when the whiskey was of equal comfort. Oddly enough, many of those times seemed to be when he and Sarah were together.

He poured golden liquid into a pair of shot glasses, taking care not to spill any.

"I half hope he is," he said defiantly. "I'd sure as hell chip in an ounce of dust for a little protection. Then maybe we could get through a week without having to spend half our time putting our lives back together again courtesy of Lahood's riders."

Sarah sniffed disapprovingly. "Protection? You expect protection from a hired killer?"

Hull whirled, trying to follow this leap of logic. "How do you know that's what he is?"

"How do *you* know that's what he *isn't*?" Having made what was obviously the definitive statement on the subject, she turned to her daughter. "Come on, Megan. We're going home." Furiously, she began dumping the bowls of stew back into the kettle. Hull set the bottle and untouched whiskey aside and put both arms around her in what he hoped would be interpreted as a conciliatory gesture.

"Sarah, I never said that he—"

"Then get rid of him! Maybe we have to deal with his kind when Lahood sends them riding through the canyon, but at least we don't have to live with that kind of trash. Get rid of him."

"I will. I promise, I—"

"Today!"

"Sure, right after supper. I'll—"

"No, not after supper. Now!"

"Sarah." Hull tried to reason with her. "He saved me from McGill and his men. If it weren't for him I'd be lying in Blankenship's back room right now with Curley the barber tryin' to fix broken bones. I invited him up here. I can't just up and kick him out into the cold."

"I won't break bread with that kind of man, Hull Barret. I don't care what he did for you, and I don't wonder that he did it for reasons of his own. You go and tell him that—"

The door to the back room swung wide. The stranger stood there in the portal, minus his mackinaw and veiled in shadow. When he spoke he sounded mildly amused.

"Hope I'm not the cause of all the excitement here."

He stepped out into the front room, filling it with his bulk. No one said anything. They just stood and stared. Spotting the twin glasses full of fine whiskey that reposed on the table, he walked over to it and nodded his thanks.

"Don't mind if I do."

Lifting one shot glass, he drained the contents at a gulp. Neat and clean, and without wiping his lips with the back of his hand.

By the expressions on the faces of the cabin's other occupants, you would've thought a bear had just come wandering into the cabin. Hull was as dumbfounded as Sarah and Megan. Come to think of it, an intruding bear he would have known how to react to, but this—this was as unexpected as the stranger's first appearance back in town.

The half-expected Colt did not hang from his belt. There wasn't even a knife. What he wore instead was a dark wool shirt surmounted by the bright white starched collar of a minister.

The silence in the room persisted until he spoke again

"Nothing like a shot of whiskey to whet a man's appetite. Going to be cold out tonight, too. Winter's coming." He indicated the steaming kettle. "Fine-looking fricassee you've cooked up there, ma'am. Don't want to let it get cold."

Sarah Wheeler couldn't move. She was paralyzed by her recent outburst and the certain knowledge that he must surely have overheard. Somehow she pulled free of Hull's embrace and stood there fighting to regain her composure.

"I apologize. For what I said. If you heard, I mean, I guess I—I didn't realize that—"

"I'll be damned," Hull muttered tersely. Then he realized what he'd said and who he'd said it to and coughed, trying to smother the sudden blasphemy. He had as much reason as Sarah to be embarrassed by the visitor's unexpected revelation, if only for the thoughts he'd been entertaining with regard to the man's profession.

It seemed that the only one capable of movement was Megan. She almost fell over herself in her eagerness to pick up the wooden ladle. Hastily she began spooning the thick stew back into the four bowls. She conveyed the largest of these to the Preacher, moving with all the speed of an Untouchable in the service of a raj. Her lips were working almost as fast as her hands.

"There—and here's some biscuits," she said rapidly as she flew around the kitchen area, "and salt, and honey for the biscuits, and—you want anything else?" She stepped to one side, pausing to catch her breath while eyeing the visitor with praise-hungry eyes.

He rewarded her with a wide grin that illuminated the room almost as effectively as the setting sun. "Well, maybe some company. Been a month since I shared my supper with anything but a horse." He glanced mischievously over at Hull and Sarah. "You folks join us?"

Megan continued adding items to the table as they occurred to her. "Ma? Hull?" Condiments and biscuits continued piling up around the Preacher, who had yet to begin eating.

"Why, of course." As the shock wore off, Sarah struggled to conceal her nervousness. It had been such a long time since she'd had dinner with, well, with anyone besides a miner, and she was desperately afraid of saying the wrong thing.

But then, she told herself as she felt herself flush, she'd done that already, hadn't she?

"How do you do? And thank you for your help on Hull's behalf today. I should've thanked you before this. It's inexcusable. I'm Sarah Wheeler. My daughter, Megan."

"Pleased to make your acquaintance, ladies."

If Sarah was embarrassed, Hull was both embarrassed and confused.

"Guess I kind of got carried away, there. With what I was thinkin', and all. The way you handled those men in town, I never would've thought you'd be a—"

Megan interrupted him, smiling at their guest. "Will you say Grace?" She sat down next to him and bowed her head, pressing her fingers together. The Preacher looked inquiringly at Sarah and Hull, who settled into the remaining chairs and lowered their eyes respectfully.

"Father, we thank Thee for these good friends, and for the bounty of the rich earth which Thee hast bestowed on us. We thank Thee for Thy many blessings; for the bountiful game and the fruits of the soil, for the good water and the long summer. For what we are about to receive, may we be truly thankful." He concluded the prayer without noticing the way

Megan was looking at him. Her eyes were shining as he reached for his spoon.

'A-men,'' she said firmly.

Maybe her mother was embarrassed, and maybe Hull was disappointed, but not Megan. She knew a miracle when she met one.

IV

A cannon that spat water instead of fire was not a sign, as one might think, that the world had been turned topsy-turvy. For one thing, its blast was just as destructive as any weapon in the army's arsenal, and considerably more consistent.

Mounted atop its wooden platform, the water cannon (also known as a monitor) utilized the diverted flow of the devastated canyon's stream to literally shake the earth loose from its banks. Above the monitor's reach all was serene and unchanged where the creek flowed rough and undisturbed over a rocky bottom. Spruces and pines lined the shore, interspersed with smaller growth like ironwood and live oak.

Below the platform, where the monitor had been doing its work for weeks, the canyon might as well have been on the eastern side of the moon instead of the golden gate. Where the powerful stream of water had ripped the canyon's flanks to shreds nothing remained but bare rock. Every living thing, every shrub and flower, down to the last ounce of topsoil, had been torn loose and flushed downstream.

The operators of the monitor were not interested in living

things. They wanted to see only the gold-bearing gravel that lined the creek. Two dozen sweating, muscular workers, many stripped to the waist, labored endlessly to shovel the dislodged stone into the upper end of a forty-foot-long iron sluice. Not all the water was taken from the creek to power the monitor. Some was used to wash the gravel down the long iron ramp, where it was kicked and tumbled over metal grids of diminishing size.

Inspecting the sluice's bounty was a rakishly handsome young man of twenty-five. He paid no attention to the spray-drenched laborers, treating them with only slightly less disdain than he reserved for immigrants, slaves, and household vermin. He could do this to men better and stronger than himself because of an accident of nature. It was his fortune to have been born to the name Lahood.

Something drew his attention away from the gold-gleaning riffles that lined the bottom of the sluice. Three men drew near enough for him to recognize them. Josh Lahood let out an oath and went to meet them.

All three wore crude bandages. Jagou and Tyson had white cloth wrapped around their heads, while a thick roll of absorbent cotton had been secured to McGill's lower jaw. They reined in when they saw Lahood was coming to meet them. The boss's son had to raise his voice in order to make himself heard above the rumble of the monitor. It didn't take much of an effort. He was plenty mad.

"Where the hell have you three been? Your shift began an hour ago. You think I'm gonna leave Club on the monitor forever?"

Tyson and Jagou said nothing, leaving it to McGill to explain as best he was able. " 'Pologize, Josh. We'd've been here on time but we got tied up at the sawbones."

"Lucky thing he was visitin' his sister, too," Jagou mumbled.

Lahood scrutinized their assortment of bandages, and took note of their subdued attitude. Neither was appropriate to this trio. They were among his daddy's toughest and most inspired hell-raisers.

"I can see that. The three of you look like you fell down a mine shaft. What the hell happened?"

McGill had trouble with the words, was rescued by the reluctant Tyson. "Well, we were takin' it easy-like outside the office, boss, killin' time until it was our turn on shift, and Barret rode into town. You remember how we did him last time he tried that?"

"Yeah, I remember. So?"

"Well, we had a little set-to. Just funnin' him a little, and—"

"Wait a minute." Lahood's gaze narrowed as he looked from one battered visage to the other. "I want to be sure I understand what you're saying. You got yourselves whipped? All three of you, in Lahood, California? By a lousy tin-pan?"

"Oh no, Boss, not just him!"

"He had some of those other dirt-grubbers from Carbon with him?"

"Well, not exactly. See, there was this stranger kinda gave him a hand, and we—"

"What stranger?" Lahood frowned. Something here didn't make sense. "Who are you talking about? If he wasn't from Carbon, then where'd he come from?"

Fed up with the whole embarrassing business, McGill was in no mood to go into details. But with the boss's son standing there glaring back at him he couldn't play dumb.

"Blankenship's."

Lahood gave him a jaundiced eye. "That's not what I mean and you know it, McGill."

"We didn't see him coming. He left with Barret. Didn't stick around to chat, and that suited us fine. Never did get his name."

"No? Looks to me like he left each of you his calling card." The three roustabouts exchanged sheepish looks. Each man fervently wished he'd come to work early instead of loafing around town looking for a little excitement. They'd found more than they'd bargained for.

"*One* stranger?" Lahood inquired. McGill nodded.

The pistol slung at the younger man's hip caught the sun as he turned away. "That's just great." He didn't try to keep the disgust out of his voice. "Dad's goin' to be thrilled when he hears about this." The trio looked more miserable than ever, but Lahood wasn't finished with them yet.

"McGill, take over the sluice."

The foreman put a hand to his aching jaw. "Boss, I ain't sure I—"

"Well I *am* sure. Get your ass over there. Tyson, Jagou— you two get to work the monitor."

Tyson groaned and shared a look of misery with his friend as the two of them followed Lahood up the hill. Working the monitor was the hardest job in camp, because it wanted to go everywhere except where you wanted it to. You had to lean on it constantly, using all your strength, and at the end of a shift with the water cannon every muscle in your body ached. McGill stood alone for a moment, watching them go. Then he slunk over toward the sluice and tried to make himself vanish in the spray.

Up atop the monitor platform, Lahood rapped the man everyone called Club on the shoulder. He had to stand on his tiptoes to do it. Club was well over seven feet tall and broad in proportion. He was the only man in camp, maybe in all of northern California, who could handle a raging monitor all by himself. Jagou and Tyson would have to wrestle with it for awhile. Lahood had another job in mind for the giant.

Nowhere in the world does the morning dawn as bright and clear as it does in the Sierra Nevada. Not for nothing had the exploring Spaniards christened it the Range of Light. Something in the air combined with the gray expanses of naked granite to produce an alpenglow distinctive among the mountain ranges of the Earth.

Hull emerged from his cabin, arched his back, and inhaled deeply of the fresh alpine air. As he started downslope toward his claim, he reached automatically for the heavy sledgehammer that stood propped up against the cabin's outer wall.

This morning was different from those previous, because today he had company. Hull was glad of the Preacher's presence. Not only was he apparently willing to keep the miner company, perhaps Hull could also induce him to say a prayer or two. The way the digging had been going lately he could use all the help he could get, and he was not a man to exclude the possible influence of the ecclesiastical.

"This man Lahood," the Preacher asked him conversationally, "I take it he's the one you folks have been feuding with?"

Hull nodded brusquely. "Him and his son. Those were their boys you knocked off me in town yesterday. Old Coy Lahood's one of the most powerful men in this part of the country. I guess he come up here in '54, '55. One of the first miners to figure out that the original placer deposits in the American River were played out and to start poking his way up into these tributaries. I reckon he was just about the first man up in these parts to really strike it rich."

The canyon was alive with activity as the two men picked their way down to the creekbed. Work was evenly divided between those fortunate few who had been spared the attention of Lahood's riders and those who were laboring hard to repair the damage that had been done to their equipment by the rampaging horsemen.

There was also a third group busy at a different task entirely. Several men were loading their families and all their worldly possessions onto the backs of sway-backed mules or into flimsy wagons. Lahood had beaten down a few more of Hull's neighbors. He was dismayed to see how many there were this morning. He'd hoped Ulrik Lindquist's defection the previous evening might prove an isolated one.

He kept his depression to himself. What right did he have to burden the Preacher with his problems? No doubt a traveling man of the cloth carried around worries of his own.

As if sensing his distress, the tall man urged him to continue with his story.

"Well, Lahood, he'd save himself a poke instead of blowin' it on gamblin' and women, and he'd use it to buy into new claims. One way or another he'd end up losin' his partners after a month or two. He'd buy 'em out, or scare 'em out, and there's tell one was found floatin' down the river. But there's not much law in this part of the country and there was less back then, and couldn't nobody never prove nothin' on the old man.

"He'd settle into each new claim and mine it out, save the proceeds, and buy into some more. Kept at it until he had himself enough to float a proper company. Last couple of years he's gone at it in a big way. Uses them hydraulic monitors. Water cannons—you ever seen one?" The Preacher nodded. "Then you've seen what they do. They blast the

place where they're workin' all to hell—excuse my French—
and when they move on, the place where they've been at ain't
worth nothin' no more to man or beast. Can't nothin' live in a
canyon that's been mined with a monitor.

"But they've made Lahood richer than ever. Carbon Canyon's about the only part of this ridge his crew hasn't ruined
yet. It's drivin' him crazy because we're right in the middle
of where he's been workin'. He's blasted out all the little
creeks all around Carbon, but this stream's the biggest in
these hills and a bunch of the others all feed into it. Engineer
fella in Placerville once told me Carbon's even on the map."

The Preacher looked thoughtful. "No wonder he wants you
folks out of here."

Hull nodded. "If there's more than trace gold in these
hills, I figure it's got to be here in Carbon. So does Spider
and the rest of the old-timers. But it's gettin' harder and
harder for them to stick it out. Most of 'em don't cotton to
fighting. They'd rather give up and try somewheres else."

"But not you?"

"Nope, not me. And a few others, still. They all know
why Lahood wants their claims."

"He's greedy for it," said a new voice.

Glancing over a shoulder, the Preacher saw that Megan had
elected to tag along behind them. She was following at a
respectful distance, but clearly still near enough to overhear.
He acknowledged her presence with a half grin and was
rewarded with a smile that traveled from ear to dainty ear. He
turned his attention back to his host.

"You're clear enough about Lahood being anxious. Does
he have any lawful rights to the canyon?"

Hull shook his head, and a hint of pride crept into his
voice. "Not enough for an ant to piss on. My claim's filed

proper in Sacramento, same as everybody else's here. Bunch of us checked this creek out, had a long chat with Spider Conway, and decided to settle in here. We rode into Sacramento in a body and filed together. Can't nobody say my claim or Cobbler's or anybody else's ain't legal, 'cause we're all witness to each other's filin'.

"So far Lahood's only been able to scare people out. But if many more leave, then he'll start buyin' up their claims and that'll force the rest of us out. He'll move in here with his crew and his machines and his damn monitor, and those of us who don't sell out to him won't have a chance. All we'll get in our pans and sluices is gravel.

"Right now the only way Lahood can legally get his hands on this land is if most of us abandon it. You probably know you can't keep title to a claim unless somebody's workin' it."

The Preacher nodded and commented wryly, "I guess he's been kind of persuasive, hasn't he?" He gestured in the direction of those men who were packing to leave.

"I don't care if all of 'em quit." Megan kicked a rock aside and spoke as she trailed along behind them. "I'm staying. Lahood killed my dog. And my grandpa, too. They can't make *me* leave."

At the mention of the death, the Preacher's face assumed a darker expression. "No lawman in town? No one you can take your case to? Town's big enough to rate a sheriff."

Hull laughed derisively. "If there was one, Lahood'd own him like he owns practically everything else. He'd been the one most likely to do the payin', so he'd end up nominatin' himself to do the hirin'. I ain't met the lawman yet who'd go up against the man payin' him his wages. Not much a lawman could do anyways, even if we could find us an honest one.

Lahood ain't really killed anyone yet. He don't come near Carbon Canyon except once in a while to drool over it from on top of the ridge over there.'' He pointed to the southern crest, fringed with evergreens.

"He's mean, Lahood is, but dumb he ain't. His hired hands do all his dirty work for him. Even if somebody did get killed, some country lawman would have a heckuva time tryin' to pin it on Lahood.''

"What about what Megan just said about her grandpa?"

"Old Dad Wheeler's heart give out after one of the raids a while back. You go up to a judge and try provin' that Lahood's men caused it. He was nearly eighty." He shrugged. "I've been sort of takin' care of Sarah and Megan ever since. Not that I mind the chore, understand. If it wasn't for me they'd be long gone from here. Carbon's no place for a single woman with a child.''

He went quiet as they reached the bank of the stream. There he pretended to be studying the ground until a bored Megan sauntered off upstream. When she was well out of earshot he continued.

"It ain't that we're livin' in sin, and it ain't as if I don't want to marry the woman.''

"I can see that. What happened?"

"One day a few years back her husband—Megan's father— just lit out. Wasn't because of Lahood or anything like that. He just wasn't much good. Left her with a half-growed child. Since then, gettin' her trustful of any man has been,'' he hesitated and smiled slightly, ''well, it plain ain't been easy.'' He eyed the Preacher speculatively. ''When we do get hitched, how about you doin' the hitching?''

"If you're waiting on a woman to make up her mind, it

might be awhile. Especially going on what you've just told me."

"I know." Hull faced the creek resignedly. "It ain't as though I haven't been trying."

The Preacher reached over and took the sixteen-pound sledge from the miner's grasp. "While you're waiting, why don't you put me to work?"

"Oh, I wouldn't ask that. You're a guest here. I mean, maybe if there was something of a spiritual nature that needed taking care of in Carbon, that'd be different."

"The spirit ain't worth spit without a little hard work to firm it up. A man's body needs firming up just as much as his soul does." He swung the hammer easily with one hand, testing its heft. "You brought this down here for something besides a decoration. Tools were meant to be used. The good book's a tool. So's this. Where do we start?"

They'd reached the place where Hull's claim began. The miner led his companion over to the huge boulder that marked the center of his diggings. He let the fingers of his right hand trail over the night-chilled granite.

"I always thought that if I could split this rock and get to the gravel that's accumulated underneath I might find something. It's smack in the middle of my claim. No telling what's sifted down under it. Every time the creek floods in the spring, there's got to be a lot of stuff that gets swept under it and hung up against the base. That's how I see it, anyways.

"I figure maybe there's gold been waitin' to be found under here since the beginning of time. Big as it is, it could've been sittin' here that long, too. I've crawled all over it, and I swear there's a hairline fracture running through the whole structure. Every day for two years now, usually after Sarah and me have finished with supper, I'd come down here with the sledge and bang away at that fracture. If it is a fracture. See?''

He pointed out the spot where he'd labored so hard for so many evenings. The Preacher leaned close for a better look, and put his fingers in the shallow, uneven depression. A pitifully small portion of the giant boulder had been chipped away.

''You're right about one thing. There's sure enough a fracture there. Looks stubborn. Kind of like Sarah?''

Hull laughed gently. ''They do have something in common, don't they?'' He wore a fond expression as he inspected the unyielding surface of the monolith. ''It's like this rock and me have kind of an agreement. It's gonna do me in or I'm gonna do it in.''

''I'd be willing to lay odds on who's going to win.''

''Yeah, well, I thought of drilling it and blasting the sonofabitch. That's what Conway says I should do.'' He nodded down the creek. ''Spider Conway. I think I told you about him.''

''You mentioned his name.''

''He's been here longer than anybody else. Knows more about dirt-pan and sluice mining than anyone on this side of the Sierras, I expect, and that includes Lahood.''

The Preacher was looking past Hull and his rock now, letting his gaze roam over the steep slope just above the claim. ''But you were afraid dynamite might bring down the rimrock, right? Idly he tossed a pebble uphill.

''A lot of this is broken, and you're sitting right at the base of an old talus slope here. It'd slip pretty easy, given the right shove.''

Hull eyed him curiously. Apparently the Preacher had

dipped into other books besides the one he was required to read from on Sundays.

"Yep, that's what I figured, for sure." He tapped the boulder. "As much dynamite as it'd take to split this thing, it'd bring the whole hillside down." He nodded toward the slope above. "That'd dam up the stream, and that'd be the end of everything. I'd slow down the creek and form a lake behind it. No panning and no sluicing and all the easy gold, assuming there is any, buried under ten or twenty feet of rock and snowmelt." He stepped away from the boulder.

"Anyway, dynamite's expensive, and I don't like the idea of bein' any broker than I already am. I don't like owin' old man Blankenship or anybody else."

"Impecuniosity's not a sin," the Preacher murmured.

Hull looked at him crossways. "What?"

"Nothing. Let's have a look at the whole project."

Following Hull's lead, the two men circled the boulder. When they had completed their geological circumnavigation the Preacher rolled up his sleeves, spit into one palm, and rubbed both hands together. It was the first time Hull had gotten a good close look at those hands. One thing was immediately apparent: they had handled rougher material than the leather exterior of a bible.

"There's plain few problems," the tall man said as he raised the sledge over his head, "that can't be solved by application of a little sweat and hard work."

The sledge seemed to hang in the air for a moment, the iron head suddenly weightless against the sun. Then it descended. The resultant *clang* reverberated the length of the canyon.

Two cousins, prospectors since the first strike back in '49, heard the sound and looked curiously toward its source. Jake and Hilda Henderson paused in the process of strapping a washtub and rocking chair onto the back of their rickety wagon to look down at Hull Barret's claim. Up the hillside a young recently married couple turned away from the open steamer trunk they'd been filling with clothes to peer curiously out their wax-paper window.

Hull watched the Preacher work, admiring the smooth, apparently effortless swings of his long arms. Then he turned to study the wreckage of his placer cradle. Legs needed to be straightened and one would have to be replaced. He could get down to the dull but necessary work of repairing the rocker as he'd intended, or . . .

Maybe it was the Preacher's quiet enthusiasm, the energy he was putting into his efforts. Or maybe it was the thought of him challenging the impossible. Whatever it was, it infected Hull as well. There was a second sledge lying amidst the splintered wood of the sluice. Hull picked it up and checked the handle. It was older than the one the Preacher was wielding, but still serviceable. Hard to break a good sledge. Or a good man.

Taking up a stance opposite the Preacher, he waited for an opening and then swung. Now the sounds of steel on rock rang out across the canyon in ragged syncopation at twice the rate, the two men driving the metal against the rock like a pair of Irishmen driving spikes into rails.

Megan had turned back and now gazed at them admiringly, until something further downstream caught her attention. It took a moment before she recognized the approaching riders. Then she ran toward the two men.

"Hull! Mr—Mr. Preacher!"

The steady hammering of the sledges ceased, and they both looked up at her, then turned their gazes in the direction she was pointing.

ALAN DEAN FOSTER

Josh Lahood was less than twenty yards away and coming straight toward them. He was not alone. Riding alongside him was a man whose legs nearly touched the ground on either side of his laboring mount.

Megan moved to stand close to the Preacher, clutching his arm as if for protection. Leaning on his sledge, the tall man spoke to Hull without taking his eyes from the approaching riders.

"Anyone you know?"

Hull wiped the sweat from his forehead. His expression was grim. " 'Fraid so. The one on the left is Lahood's boy, Josh. The other one," and he shook his head, his voice hushed. "I've never seen him before. I can swear to that. Must be new with Lahood's operation. If I'd seen him before I'm damn sure I wouldn't have forgotten him."

The horses slowed and came to a halt nearby. Josh Lahood leaned forward, his crossed arms resting on his mount's neck, and favored them with a thin smile.

"Afternoon, Barret—Megan."

His smile widened when he turned it on her. An indifferent fate had blessed Josh Lahood with an inordinate share of immature good looks, when better men than he went begging among the ladies. To make matters worse, he was well aware of the fact. At once attracted and repelled, Megan responded to his ingratiating grin with a curt nod.

Having concluded the amenities as quickly as possible, Lahood now turned his attention to the tall stranger standing next to the girl. "Friend of yours, Barret? Don't think I've seen him around town before."

"No, he just came in," Hull explained. He hesitated long enough to cast a glance in his friend's direction before plunging on. "He's our new Preacher."

66

An undecipherable noise emerged from between the giant's lips, an eloquent hiss that effectively conveyed his feelings.

"Preacher, huh?" Lahood gazed speculatively at the tall man. The subject of his attention did not reply, save to favor the younger Lahood with a benign smile.

A fair number of the canyon's inhabitants were witness to this confrontation. No one thought to intervene. None were really capable of it, frozen as they were by the very idea. You didn't stand up to Josh Lahood. You just tried to stay out of his way. The miners and their kind couldn't have been more astonished by what they were seeing than if the sun had chosen to rise that morning in the west.

After a moment, Jake Henderson shushed his wife and resumed the work of securing the old rocker to the wagon. A few of his neighbors echoed his action, but not all. Some found themselves unable to turn away from the little drama that was taking place over at the Barret claim. It was not unlike watching a rattler preparing to strike: the outcome was preordained, but the movements were fascinating.

"Hear you messed up some of my men yesterday, Preach," Lahood said flatly.

"Nothing personal. And I didn't know they were your men. I thought they were your daddy's men."

Lahood flushed angrily while Club merely allowed himself a second grunt of contempt.

"Nothing personal, eh? Then maybe you won't take it personal if we tell you to leave Carbon Canyon."

The Preacher scuffed at the gravel with one foot before gazing thoughtfully up at Lahood. "There's a lot of sinners hereabouts. You wouldn't want me to leave before I was done with my work, would you?"

Club looked toward his employer for instructions. Lahood

considered the situation a moment longer, then sighed with exaggerated reluctance and nodded once. The giant grinned as he slid down off his mount.

By now nearly everyone in the canyon had put aside their work to gaze in fascination at what was happening down on the creek. Sarah Wheeler was among them. She was unable to follow the distant conversation, but when Club dismounted the color drained from her face.

Spider Conway was standing on the porch of his shanty, watching. Now he let go a squirt of tobacco juice at a beetle sunning itself on a nearby rock and shook his head sadly.

Anchored by the Preacher. Hull held his ground as the giant came toward them. He stopped less than a yard away, forcing the two men to tilt their heads back in order to meet his gaze. It was dead quiet save for the musical warbling of the creek.

When it became clear neither the tin-pan nor his friend were about to retreat, the giant decided a more active demonstration was required. With a single sweep of one massive arm he reached out to snatch Hull's sledge from his grasp. In the same motion he lifted it over his head.

Hull tensed, ready to make a run for it, but it was immediately apparent the blow wasn't aimed in his direction. The Preacher simply smiled and watched. Club turned and brought the sledge down with incalculable force right in the depression the miner had chipped out of the boulder.

There was an explosive *c r a c k!* The mammoth stone shuddered once. Then it split in two, dust rising from the gap. The two halves rocked back and forth as they settled into place.

The recoil from the blow stunned the man who'd delivered it, and Club needed a minute to recover his balance. Gripping the sledge firmly in both hands, he turned a disdainful glare on the Preacher.

Lolling in his saddle, Lahood made use of the same dry, casual tone he'd employed previously. "Your work about done now, Preach?"

The tall man eyed the cloven rock with apparent indifference. "Part of it, leastways."

Stubborn, Lahood mused. Too bad. He nodded to the giant. Club's fingers tightened on the sledge. With a gesture as casual as a caress, the Preacher pushed Megan away from him. Hull retreated cautiously, uncertain what to do next and fearful of what was coming. If the Preacher asked him, he'd make a dash for his shovel, or the old rifle up in his cabin. But the tall man said nothing, just stood and watched his oversized opponent.

Up on his porch Spider Conway's jaw dropped as he sensed what was coming. "Jessuusss," he mumbled.

The two men took each other's measure for a long moment. Then Club let out a roar that echoed down the canyon, raised the sledge over his head like a shillelagh, and charged...

... straight into the outstretched end of the Preacher's hammer, which flattened the giant's nose like a boot heel flattening a horse apple.

Club straightened up and staggered backward. Blood oozed from his nose as the Preacher casually brought his weapon around and up lightly, to catch the giant square between his legs. Club immediately bent double, letting go of his own hammer and suddenly unconcerned with any threat a theological invasion might pose to his employer's interests. He was entirely concerned about his own interests.

The Preacher tossed the sledge aside and stepped forward, not to strike again but to hook an arm beneath the giant's and help him stagger toward his horse. As they walked he whispered to his erstwhile assailant. There was no malice in his voice, not any hint of gloating. Only concern for another man's well-being.

"A little ice'll help ease the pain. You'll be fine by morning. Here we go, foot in the stirrup, that's right. Now right leg up and over, push there, attaboy."

With a heave he helped deposit the giant on his horse side-saddle. Then he turned and bestowed upon the gaping Josh Lahood a properly ecclesiastical gesture of farewell.

"Thanks for stopping by, son. Always willing to have a chat."

Just then Lahood didn't look quite as handsome as usual. His face was twisted into a florid mask of hate. His hand started to descend toward the gun that rode on his hip.

His fingers froze as the Preacher's gaze suddenly narrowed. His expression, no longer benign, had unexpectedly metamorphosed into something quite different. No one else saw it, not Hull, not Megan. It was intended for and noticed only by Josh Lahood.

There was no reason for the younger man not to draw. No reason at all. And yet—there was something in the tall man's eyes, something long buried and well hidden that hadn't shown itself until this moment. Whatever it was, it caused Lahood's hand to halt an inch above the pistol grip. It hung there for a long moment, suspended by something powerful and undefinable.

Then Lahood blinked like a man who'd been lulled to sleep. He wiped the back of a hand across his eyes and glanced at the Preacher one more time. With a yelp of confusion and frustration, he wrenched his animal around and started back the way he'd come. Club's horse turned to follow instinctively, the giant's massive but inert form slumped in the saddle.

Up on her porch Sarah Wheeler suddenly remembered to breathe as she steadied herself against a post. She hadn't moved a muscle from the time Club had climbed down off his horse until he and Josh Lahood had turned to ride out of the canyon.

As soon as Lahood was out of pistol range, the Preacher bent to retrieve his discarded sledge. Hull and Megan stared at him as if transfixed. He ignored them as he walked over to examine the broken halves of the giant boulder. Hull had been right about the fracture.

"Well now," he murmured as he examined the by-product of Club's demonstration, "the Lord does work in mysterious ways."

Clang! The sledge described a sweeping arc through the clear morning air and struck one half of the split rock. The half trembled, then fell into two pieces. Grinning, Hull hurried to pick up his own sledge, the one the giant had taken away from him. For the second time that morning the double echo of iron on granite rang throughout the canyon.

Spider Conway let loose with another burst of dark juice, grinning around the chaw tucked in his left cheek. "Preacher my ass," he said aloud, looking thoughtful. "But then, Christ didn't look like no carpenter, neither."

There was a pile of old tools stacked neatly outside the door. On impulse he reached down and picked up his own, slightly smaller sledgehammer. Then he loped down the steps, heading for the creekbed.

He was the first, but not the last. From cabins and shanties, from behind wagons and sheds, singly at first and then in pairs and trios, the other miners put aside their fears, ceased preparing to abandon their homes and claims, and hurried to join the two men who were battering the recalcitrant granite with steady blows of their sledges. Henderson was the last, the rocker and wagon forgotten along with any thoughts of flight. There was new hope in Carbon Canyon. It showed itself in the joyful faces of the men as they pounded away at the shrinking sections of the boulder and threw the smaller fragments aside. Of course it wasn't just stone they were destroying and tossing aside: it was their own fears and despair. They all but sang as they worked.

Megan moved clear of the busy men and the flying shards of stone, and found a place close to the water where she could sit and watch. Her face was alive with pleasure and contentment, and never more so than when it focused on the tall man who was working hardest of all. The sunlight gleamed on the white collar that ringed his neck.

V

The train's whistle rose to a shriek as it rounded the curve that had been laboriously hacked out of the mountainside. White smoke stained the air above its funnel, then quickly turned black as it fell behind the engine. Soot marred the cars it pulled, impairing the clarity of the thick glass windows.

It was slowing rapidly as it approached the tiny wooden building that served as a station. Above this unimpressive structure was a neatly painted sign that proclaimed to anyone with a view (who was also capable of reading) that they had just arrived at

LAHOOD, CALIFORNIA—POP. 189

The platform in front of the station was deserted, but there was a greeting committee of sorts waiting nearby. Three horses and two men stood in the shade of the big oak that grew just to the north of the station. The saddled horse that stood patiently between Josh Lahood and McGill's mounts was intended for one of the train's passengers. Its only important passenger, as far as anyone in Lahood, California, was concerned. Josh held the reins of the riderless mount and tried to pick out a certain face from the many visible through the dusty windows.

The riderless animal was a gleaming black Arabian, an aristocrat among the four-legged serfs who dominated this part of the equine world. The saddle blanket that protected its expensive back was fashioned of the finest crimson-dyed wool, while the saddle itself was an exquisitely tooled curve of fine leather chased with silver. Once it had cushioned the pampered backside of a Mexican don. American squatters and American law had devastated his hacienda. Eventually he had also lost his saddle, to an equally wealthy if considerably more ruthless and less cultured rider.

The stationmaster emerged from the stationhouse. He was a feisty, independent character who'd given up mining for a steady job, something that becomes particularly attractive to a man when he passes fifty. The trainman tossed him a small canvas mailbag and squinted at his colleague.

"Mornin', Whitey. Any mail goin' south?"

"Not today, Jake. Had a couple letters for a fella down in Mariposa, but a friend came through and offered to take them

73

to his mate personal. Nothin' else—unless you want to tell the President what I think of him.''

While the two men chatted, a black porter stepped off the first car behind the mailcar. One hand held a valise while the other reached up to aid a departing passenger.

''Watch de step, Mr. Lahood.''

''Why?'' a sharp, no-nonsense voice wanted to know. ''Has the damned thing moved since we left Sacramento?''

Coy Lahood ignored the proferred hand and hopped off the train. Retrieving his bag from the porter, he pressed a folded bill into the man's hand. Sixty-two, with swept-back silver hair, square jaw, and a spine as straight as a clipper ship's mainmast, he looked quite out of place in his neatly pressed three-piece suit, complete to pearl buttons and gold watch fob.

''Thanks, Mr. Lahood, suh.'' The porter mounted the first step and leaned out to wave up the line. The engineer responded with a wave of his own and a blast from the engine's whistle.

Josh Lahood dismounted and hurried to greet his father.

''I'll take your bag, Papa.'' The elder Lahood handed over the valise, acknowledging his offspring with a perfunctory nod.

''Morning, son. McGill.''

The foreman touched the brim of his hat with an index finger. ''Morning, Boss. Good to have you back. How was Sacramento?''

Lahood's reply sounded wistful. ''Paradise. Would've stayed another week if I thought I could've spared the time. Two politicians for every Chinese laundry, two whores for every politician. Some of the whores as sweet smelling and clean as the laundry.'' McGill and the younger Lahood chuckled dutifully at the old man's joke. "Good food, smart talk about gold and politics and anything else a man might care to discourse on. Civilization."

"Sounds like fun, Boss."

Lahood eyed his foreman and shook his head sadly. "It's more than that, McGill, but I don't expect you to understand what I'm talking about. I'll say this about Sacramento: if there was gold in the Delta, I'd move there permanently. That, and if they'd figure out a way to get rid of the damn mosquitoes."

A second whistle, then the train behind them began to move, inching its way toward the next whistle-stop. Lahood patted his mount affectionately on its neck, then swung himself up into the saddle. He moved with the suppleness of a man half his age.

"How was business in Sacramento, Papa?"

"Well, I didn't do us any harm and I might've done us some good. We'll know when this session of the Legislature finishes its work. How's business here?" He slapped the reins gently against the horse's neck. Flanked by his son and foreman, Lahood headed toward his town.

"Still pulling low-grade ore out of number-five shaft, but the vein's about played out."

Lahood nodded; he didn't seem surprised. "Uh-huh. I figured as much before I left. What else?"

"We went another twenty feet in the twelve-shaft, pulled out nothing but magnetite, and shut her down. McKenzie came runnin' out of ten this morning screaming he'd found the mother lode and waving what looked like the biggest nugget of all time." The foreman spat into dust. "Pyrite. That's what comes of hirin' so many new men. Don't know a damn thing about mining.

"Anyways, I kicked his worthless ass all the way down the river. Gettin' everyone all excited like that. Main problem is that the placer vein in Cobalt Canyon's wearin' thin, too. We're washing out three times as much dirt and rock for half the gold we were gettin' when we set up in there."

"None of which is unexpected. Be nice if the gold in each canyon would last forever, but it doesn't work that way." His tone altered slightly but significantly. "What about Carbon?"

His son hesitated until the elder Lahood's gaze began to narrow. "Well, we ran another raid through Carbon couple days back. Busted up everthing in sight and threw a real good scare into 'em. Didn't we, McGill? Had those tin-pans running like chickens for their coops."

"Yep, sure did." The foreman's enthusiasm was muted. "Almost drove 'em out this time lock, stock, and barrel. You could see some of 'em startin' to pack up by the time we hit the west ridge."

"Uh-huh." Lahood acknowledged this information without turning his eyes from the road leading into town. When further elaboration was not forthcoming he repeated himself, rather more emphatically this time.

"Uh-huh?"

McGill looked helplessly over at the younger Lahood, who tried to find the right words. Somehow explaining things to his father was never as easy as berating the men.

"Something happened that we didn't anticipate. It seems this stranger wandered in. Sort of pulled them together, kind of." He glanced quickly at the foreman. "That the way you see it, McGill?"

"Yep. He sort of—pulled 'em together."

"Pulled them together? Sort of kind of?" Lahood looked at his foreman, then back to his son. "How—with a lariat? You boys are full of interesting information today, ain't you? You just ain't much on explanations.''

Josh Lahood swallowed. ''I don't know how he did it, Papa. They just sort of seemed to get strength from him.''

''This one stranger did that? I thought that Barret was the leader of the squatters.''

''We took care of Barret. Would've had him buffaloed good and proper if this stranger hadn't come along.'' McGill's explanation sounded lame even to himself.

Lahood shook his head in disbelief. ''Hell, I expect you boys didn't explain to him just who we are and how we work things around here. I imagine that once you 'explain' things to him, he'll decide to move on.''

His son's laugh was brittle. ''Sure! Ain't much for a preacher to do in these parts, after all. Ain't many churchgoers in these camps.''

Lahood reined up abruptly. His expression was dark. The relaxed, easy-going man who'd stepped off the train had suddenly changed into something far less pleasant.

''Preacher!?'' His voice dropped dangerously. ''You cretins let a *preacher* into Carbon Canyon?''

Josh looked helpless, and not a little confused by his father's outburst. ''Hell, we didn't invite him, Papa. I don't know that anybody invited him. He just showed up one day and sort of took up with Barret, is all. Wasn't anything we could do about it. I don't see what you're so all-fired upset about. What's so dangerous about a preacher?''

You're your mother's son for sure, Lahood thought disgustedly. Can't see beyond the tip of your nose.

''When I left for Sacramento those tin-pans had all but given up. They were just about ready to call it quits in Carbon, and I thought I'd get back here all set for us to move in. Their spirit was nearly broken, and a man without spirit is whipped.

"But a preacher, he could give 'em faith. Shit, one ounce of faith and they'll be dug in deeper than ticks on a hound." He considered the problem for a long moment, then flicked the reins. The Arabian obediently started forward again.

Josh Lahood rode in silence next to his father for as long as he thought prudent before asking, "So what do we do about him, Papa?"

Lahood, who'd been on the verge of exploding only moments ago, now seemed his old relaxed self once more. "I expect I'm going to have to talk to this fellow myself. You boys go throw a rope around that man and bring him to me."

Josh and McGill exchanged a glance. Just about anything else the elder Lahood could have suggested would have been more to their liking. Both had already suffered embarrassment at the stranger's hands. Neither had any wish to repeat the experience. But there wasn't a thing they could do. Coy Lahood had given them an order.

Their silence saved them from themselves. To their great relief, the old man changed his mind. "No. On second thought, if we get too rough, we'll make a martyr out of him. Don't want to give them a martyr. A dead preacher can be more dangerous than a live one."

"Didn't you get any help from Sacramento, boss?" McGill inquired hesitantly, anxious to divert the conversation away from the subject of the Preacher.

"Sacramento? Sacramento ain't worth moose piss!" the elder Lahood snorted derisively. "Sometimes I think things were better when the Mexicans were running the territory." He gazed thoughtfully down at his silvered saddle. "It's easier to do business with people when they're running scared. Them bastards in Sacramento are all pumped up with themselves. Every one of 'em thinks he's going to be a United States senator one of these days, and you can't talk sense to any of 'em.''

"They didn't sign the writ?" Josh looked surprised.

"Nope. Not only that, but there's talk of much worse.''

His son frowned. "What are you talking about, Papa?"

"It's hard to believe, but some of those dumb politicians want to do away with hydraulic mining altogether. 'Raping the land,' they call it.''

Josh's eyes widened. "That's just talk, ain't it, Papa? They can't do something like that.''

"No telling what a bunch of politicians will do when you put 'em all together. They start listening to each other's speeches. You weren't in Sacramento with me, boy. Things are changing. It ain't like the old days when I was getting started.

"The farmers, them dumb dirt-scrabblers, are putting their own lobby together, and every month there's a few more farmers and a few less miners. They're worried about the silt from hydraulic tailings washing down into the valley and contaminating their land and crap like that.'' He shook his head sadly. "They've a mind to ruin the whole business for those of us that made this country, and those damn fool politicians just might help 'em do it. If they get paid enough.

"So far it's a standoff, but it's going to get worse for hydraulics in this state before it gets better. I've got too much invested in our setup to give it up and go back to straight shaft mining. We've got to move on Carbon and cut deep and cut fast, 'cause the way the smoke's blowing, in another couple of years we may be out of business. That's all we need anyway, is one more big strike, and I'm betting that Carbon's going to be it. Then let 'em ban hydraulic mining if they want to. We'll have enough in the bank to be able to afford to junk the equipment, raise the right kind of capital to float a really big company. We'll buy up every claim in these hills and go set ourselves up proper like I've been wanting to in Frisco. Let somebody else get their hands dirty for a change. The Lahoods'll just sit back and collect dividends.'' He looked past his son, toward the mountains that towered behind them.

"But we need to strike pay dirt in Carbon, and we need to do it fast.''

Josh and McGill rode along silently, hanging on the elder Lahood's every word.

"Those tin-pans have got to go and go this week. We can't afford to wait any longer. I want us set up in Carbon and cutting ground before the farmers' bill is put on the governor's desk, because the dumb bastard's just liable to sign it. That means that preacher has to go, too. We'll have to figure out a way to handle him.''

"Maybe we could—'' Josh began hopefully. His father cut him off.

"Shut up, boy. If you could've taken care of him you would've done so already. So keep quiet and let your old man think.''

The younger Lahood endured this criticism in silence. First, because not even blood relations talked back to Coy Lahood and second, because he knew the criticism was justified. He forced himself to say nothing during the remainder of the ride into town. After awhile he began to relax.

He was thinking of how his father was going to take care of that damn preacher man. Coy Lahood could be very inventive when the need arose. By the time they reached the outskirts of town, he was smiling.

The oak bureau had been hauled all the way from Philadelphia, around the Cape via clipper, then overland into the Sierras via wagon.

Now it reposed in the Wheeler cabin, where it constituted Sarah Wheeler's prize possession. It was the finest piece of furniture in Carbon Canyon and would have drawn appreciative comments even in Sacramento. Sarah preferred not to point it out to visitors if she could avoid doing so, however. Doing so would have meant explaining its history, and that in turn would have meant explaining how she and her former husband had come to acquire it. She preferred not to mention that man's name in her home.

On reflection, the bureau had been of more use than had the man. It stayed where it belonged, did its job, was there when she needed it, and neither beat nor berated her. Better a wooden bureau than a wooden man, she finally decided.

From time to time she wondered where he was, what he was doing. Looking for gold, no doubt, in places where a wife and a daughter would be more of an encumbrance than a help. Handsome he'd been, handsome and smooth-talking and so wise in the ways of the world. Or so he'd seemed to young Sarah. Now that she'd had a chance to experience a bit more of life she knew better. She'd mistaken vanity for confidence, lies for knowledge, and sex for love.

Not that he'd been an evil man. Just sorry, and she too young to know any better. When he'd deserted her and Megan, the hurt had been too much to bear. It was still there but healed over now, like an old break covered by new bone.

Megan was hard at work in her own room, unaware of her mother's thoughts. She was trying to pull the straps tighter against her back, the better to raise and emphasize her adolescent bosom. She turned sideways to eye herself in the beveled oval mirror, examining her half-naked form critically. It was a good figure, no doubt of that, and time would likely enhance and refine it even more. But it would've been better if she'd had someone else there to tie the corset straps for her. She didn't dare ask her mother.

What she really needed was one of those new dresses Mrs. Williams had been talking about. Mrs. Williams had been in Sacramento as recently as two months ago, to tend to her elderly sister, and had returned to Carbon Canyon full of tales of the latest in politics and fashion. The gowns she claimed to have seen sounded fit for a queen to Megan. Cut low in front, with lots of velvet and feathers, *that* was what she needed.

But all she had was the one Sunday dress, and that would have to do.

Idly she called out to the front room. "Were Grandpa and Grandma happy when you got married, Ma?"

Her mother's voice floated back to her from the kitchen. "I'm afraid they didn't have a thimbleful of choice in the matter."

Megan hardly heard the reply. She was frowning at her reflection. No matter how she altered the position of her bodice or tugged on the straps which raised the stays, she was unable to produce the desired end result with the equipment at hand.

"That's no answer. Were they surprised?"

A distant sigh. "Your grandpa took the measles and your grandma got drunk. I suppose you could say it surprised them some."

Moving to the quilt-covered bed behind her, Megan picked up the neatly laid-out gingham pinafore lying atop the covers and slipped it on over her shirtwaist. She had to do a little jig to make it slide down. No question about it, she was still growing, and the pinafore was starting to pinch in certain critical places.

"Was it 'cause they didn't think you were old enough?"

"Your grandma was only fifteen when she was married," Sarah replied. "No, I think what riled them was *who* I married. I could've been forty and they wouldn't have approved. Turns out they were both right. Too late for me to apologize now that they're both gone. I was too smart and too pig-headed to listen to the advice of a couple of old folks."

Megan adjusted the pinafore to its unsatisfactory best, then picked up her hairbrush and began working on her waist-length hair.

"Do you think you'll be happy married to Hull?"

"Who says we're getting married? Girl, you've been growing up when I wasn't looking."

Megan smiled at her reflection. "Hull's nice enough, isn't he?"

Her mother's response was deliberately flat. "Yes, he's nice."

"He likes me, and I know he likes you. Don't you like him?"

"Hull's all right. Yes, I like him, but people don't get married just because they like one another."

A dreamy cast came over Megan's face as she swayed approvingly before the mirror. "Do preachers get married?"

"I don't see why not."

That comment brought forth a broad smile from both the reflection in the mirror and its owner. A few final sharp strokes through her tresses and Megan returned the brush to its resting place atop the bureau. She all but skipped into the next room.

"Is my hem long enough?"

Sarah turned to her daughter, and Megan saw that she wasn't the only woman in the house who had been hard at work on her appearance. Her mother's long hair had been piled up into an elegant knot atop her head, where it was secured in place by tortoiseshell pins.

"Why yes. And you look lovely." Rising, she planted a kiss on her daughter's forehead. "You're the prettiest daughter I could ever have. That anyone could ever have."

Megan fidgeted under the praise while simultaneously casting an envious eye on her mother's elaborate coiffure and wondering if she could somehow manage to duplicate it. It wasn't that it made Sarah's hair any more attractive as much as it contributed to her more, well, more mature appearance, something that concerned Megan very much just now.

Hull had resurrected his Long Tom, but instead of setting it back up at the far end of his claim where it had stood originally, he'd moved it downstream. Now it stood in the lee of the pulverized boulder whose disintegration Josh Lahood's henchman had inadvertently begun.

It was strange having help. He'd worked alone for so many years he hardly knew how to handle not having to do everything himself. Of course, he was within easy shouting range of his fellow miners, but men like Conway and Miller hadn't come to the mountains to idle away their days in casual conversation. Time enough for that after sundown, when it grew too cold and dark to work.

And even then there were those in whom the gold fever ran so hot that they remained to work their claims by the light of candle and lamp.

This much the Preacher shared in common with the other sourdoughs; he preferred work to talk. Hard work at that.

Hull had to argue with the tall man before he'd let the miner take his turn at the much more strenuous job of shoveling gravel into the upper end of the sluice. Any fool could walk the Long Tom's length, searching the wooden boxes for signs of color. And when he'd protest that the Preacher was taking too long a turn with the gravel, his friend would reply that he still had five more minutes of "sermonizing with the shovel" before he'd allow Hull to take over.

He would argue, and then give in. After two years of working alone, Hull's shoulder muscles were more than a little grateful for the respite.

He was enjoying one of those breaks at the moment, busying himself with inspecting the flow of sand over the bottom of the sluice. Rocks, and more rocks, the dull gray beneath the clear water interrupted only by an occasional flash of quartz or pyrite.

Something caught his eye, masked but not obscured by the swirling water that raced the length of the sluice. The water could not obscure it. It was bright, much too bright. Much brighter than any pyrite had a right to be. He gaped at it, wiped dirt from his face, and looked again to make sure he hadn't imagined it.

Letting out a joyous whoop, he plunged his right hand into the frigid current and closed his fist over the object. It felt different from the surrounding gravel even beneath the water.

The Preacher dumped another load of gravel into the upper end of the Long Tom and paused to grin back at his friend. "You break your hand there, Barret?"

The miner had removed his fist from the water. Now he opened it to stare at what he'd retrieved. His fingers were turning pink from the cold, but he didn't feel the chill.

He turned the object over in his fingers, a rapt expression

on his face. It did not display the familiar octagonal crystal-line bulges or the surface striations common to pyrite. It was smooth and battered where the water had tumbled it across the creek bottom. And it was brighter in hue than pyrite, with a telltale reddish tinge.

"It's a nugget," he was finally able to gasp. "The biggest damn nugget I've ever seen! Look here." He let out another whoop of pure delight as he hurried to display his find.

The Preacher looked approvingly at the handful even as he echoed Hull's first thoughts. "You're sure it ain't fool's gold, now."

Hull was grinning from ear to ear. "Preacher, I've thrown away enough pyrite to plate the U.S. Capitol. Look at it. Ain't she beautiful, all smooth and polished by the water?" He rubbed one part of his find to remove the caked-on silt. His voice was hushed, reverent. "I never thought to see the like, 'cept in the papers. Always felt sure it was given to other men to make a strike like this, not Hull Barret. But you know something? Even while I was thinking that I never gave up hope." His fingers tightened around the nugget.

"I knew there was gold in this creek, and not just dust. Spider knew it, and I knew it."

"Well, don't keep it to yourself, Barret. Good news tastes best when it's shared."

"Yeah, right." He started climbing the slope, heading for the Wheeler cabin. "Hey Sarah, Megan! Have a look at this!"

Spider Conway looked up from his panning, then disgustedly tossed the contents aside as he watched Hull Barret half clamber, half run up the hillside. He directed a thin stream of tobacco juice into the mud that swirled around his ancient boots.

"It figgers." With a snort he dipped the pan again,

methodically swishing the load of sand, gravel, and water around and around, patiently letting the water remove the lighter debris as he searched for a faint trace of yellow amidst the brown, gray, and white.

His initial reaction to the discovery had been instinctive, but in reality he was quietly pleased. Hull Barret had worked as hard as anyone in Carbon Canyon, and he deserved the luck that had befallen him. Besides, better for someone to find gold than no one. It meant that the gold was there, and who knew but that maybe one day even poor old Spider Conway might find his share. He panned a little faster.

So would every man working the length of the creek, once the word got around.

Hull arrived at the cabin out of breath and breathing hard. Sarah had come out onto the porch to see what all the yelling was about and Megan now joined her.

He held his discovery out to them. It gleamed in his palm, a small lump of sun fallen to earth, and there was satisfaction as well as exultation in his voice.

"Nothing but a little dust in Carbon Canyon, Lindquist said! Nothing but dust, not worth the trouble of panning out. How's this for a piece of dust!" He turned to nod in the direction of his claim. "It came from beneath where that boulder was. I was right about that. There's all kinds of stuff sucked down under that rock that's been waitin' there for a million years, just waiting for somebody to come along and pull the cork out of the bottle." He shook it at them, his voice trembling with excitement.

"Look at it, Sarah! Look at it good. Must weigh all o' four ounces not countin' what matrix is still clinging to it. A quarter *pound* o' gold."

The nugget was roughly the size of a bird's egg, pure and

solid with only the slightest bit of quartz and sand clinging to it. It was more gold than any of them had seen in one place before, and it was all in one piece.

Impetuously Hull embraced first mother, then daughter. "How about it, Sarah? Want to celebrate?" He put his arms around her again.

"Oh Hull," Megan said hopefully, her face shining with shared excitement, "could we go into town?"

Sarah's carefully controlled approval of Hull's discovery was suddenly tempered further by the reality that underlay their lives. "I'm not sure that's such a good idea, Megan," she said slowly.

"*Please*, Mama. We've been stuck up here for ages, and if Hull thinks it's all right," she turned to the tall man who had finally joined them. "What do you think, Preacher?"

He wore that thin, enigmatic smile as he replied. "It'd sure go a ways toward clearing your credit, wouldn't it? I'm sure Mr. Blankenship would be glad to relieve you of that little burden, at a fair price. He struck me as honest enough, if a tad on the dour side."

Sarah quickly detached herself from Hull's embrace, a fact which escaped the excited Megan's notice.

Hull looked thoughtful as he considered the Preacher's words. He tossed the nugget up and down in his palm a few times, enjoying the delicious weight and feel of it while he still could. It wouldn't be his for long, and he'd be sorry to see it depart his possession, but the Preacher was right. They owed Blankenship, and the nugget would be enough to clear accounts for everybody with maybe some left over. Once their account had been cleared, they'd be able to buy on credit once more.

Besides, he told himself cockily, where there was one such nugget there were bound to be more.

"It would. It would at that. And then some."

"Gold just makes a man's pocket heavy."

Hull was grinning again. "Be worth it just to see the look on old Blankenship's face."

"Can't we go into town?" Megan asked again. "It's been so long since I've been out of the canyon."

Hull was no less realistic that Sarah. It was one of many things they shared in common. "How about it, Preacher?"

"I expect we've got as much right to go into town as anybody else."

Sarah's remaining concerns were alleviated by his choice of pronouns. "Then—you'll be coming in with us?"

The tall stranger rubbed at his right shoulder. "I don't imagine that sledge will get lonely if I let it set by itself for awhile, and I sure won't miss paying attention to *it*."

All three of them chuckled, Sarah loudest of all.

Sarah and Megan were already dressed, and it didn't take Hull long to change into a clean shirt and his spare pair of pants. Soon they were all piled into the buckboard and rattling along the creek, following the well-worn trail that led out of the canyon toward town.

Having grown bored with panning, an activity to which their limited attention spans were not naturally suited, the two Conway boys were lolling on a nearby bank. Each was whittling on a piece of white spruce, and each was trying to whittle the same thing. They looked up as the wagon jounced past.

"Goin' into town again, Mr. Barret?" Teddy called over to them.

"That's right," Hull replied. "You want to join us? Plenty of room in the back."

Eddy looked tempted and set his whittling aside. "Our daddy wouldn't let us, Mr. Barret. Says we're not to go into town without him. Says we'd like as not get ourselves into trouble." He grinned happily, a grin of utter innocence that Hull sometimes envied. "Sure is a nice day for it, though."

"Hi, Megan," Teddy called out as he spotted the younger Wheeler.

"Hello, Teddy." She sat very straight and ladylike as the buckboard passed the twins, acutely conscious of her appearance and posture. "I *do* hope you boys have a nice day."

As the wagon rattled around the next bend in the creek, Teddy Conway turned a mystified gaze on his brother. "Now what do you suppose has got into her?"

VI

The buckboard trundled down the sparsely populated main street. Most of the visitors in town were from other mining sites and did not recognize the new arrivals, but a few permanent residents did. Then they would turn their gaze down the street, staring at some unvoiced location, and increase their pace.

The two women rode in the back while the Preacher sat next to Hull on the single high bench seat. Their progress continued to draw stares from those familiar with their situation.

Among the citizens who happened to be watching the street

as the buckboard pulled up outside Blankenship's emporium was Josh Lahood. He stared at the wagon only long enough to make sure of what he was seeing before turning to vanish back inside the big warehouse that bore his name.

Hull tied the reins to the hitching rail. "I'll square things up with Blankenship. Might take a minute or two. He's liable to faint twice: once when I show him the nugget and again when I tell him it's to pay off our debts in full. When he gets over the shock maybe we'll get you an ice cream, Meg." He smiled at his tall friend. "I'll try not to be too long, Preacher. You'll keep an eye on the ladies?"

"Shouldn't be too hard," he said agreeably.

Hull grinned at him. "I'll hurry."

Buoyed by his discovery, he cleared two steps at a time in bounding up to the entrance. Meanwhile Megan's attention had been caught by movement across the street. Now she prodded the Preacher anxiously.

"Look!"

Half a dozen roughnecks had emerged from the warehouse. They paused on the porch to chat among themselves. Occasionally they would stare across the street and point. Josh Lahood followed them out but didn't stop on the boardwalk. His gun shining at his side, he strode across the street toward the wagon.

Megan's eyes darted back and forth between the approaching younger man and the Preacher. She half rose from her seat.

"I'll get Hull."

Casually, the Preacher stared her back down. "No need. He's got important business. Whether or not Mr. Blankenship keels over at the sight of the nugget, it's likely going to take them some time to square accounts. Hull's trusting, but he's nobody's fool either. Blankenship's middlin' honest, but that doesn't mean he might not try to collect extra interest on a debt long owed. Best to leave them to their figurin' and not disturb them. Reckon I may as well double-check the hitch. Appears we may be here awhile.''

Moving easily and unhurriedly, he climbed down from the seat.

Which movement prompted the roughnecks across the street to variously bend, crouch, duck, and otherwise halfway go for their guns.

If he noticed the reaction his descent provoked, the Preacher gave no sign of it. He contented himself with checking the double hitch that secured horse to rail, then turned in time to interpose himself between the buckboard and the oncoming Lahood. The younger man immediately halted a discreet ten feet away.

He glanced back toward the warehouse as if to reassure himself of his reinforcements before addressing himself stiffly to the occupants of the wagon.

''Mrs. Wheeler. Megan.'' His attention lingered a bit long on Megan, perhaps enjoying her Sunday dress, perhaps something else. Megan managed to ignore him.

He paid no attention to her now, having rapidly shifted his attention to the tall man silently confronting him. ''My father wants to see you.'' He hesitated slightly before adding, ''Now.'' His eyes locked with the Preacher, and he indicated the building across the street. There followed a very long silence, or so it seemed to Josh Lahood, anyway.

He was greatly relieved, though he never would have admitted to it, when the Preacher smiled back at him. ''I've looked forward to meeting your father.'' He glanced back at the two women. ''Hope you ladies'll pardon me for a minute or so. Hull should be out soon enough and it's not polite to refuse an invitation.''

''Don't!'' Sarah urged him in hushed tones. ''It's a trick. They just want to get you inside, away from witnesses!''

''Maybe they do, but I think it's just to talk.'' He gave her hand a reassuring pat, then started across toward the Lahood building. Josh fell in alongside, though still taking care to stay out of reach while simultaneously keeping a watch on the tall man's hands. He frowned as they walked, unable to reconcile the absence of visible weapons or the presence of the white collar with the story McGill and his men had told.

Both Wheeler women watched their progress.

''What if they hurt him?'' Megan's voice was full of apprehension. ''What if they—?''

''*Shut up, Megan,*'' her mother said tightly.

Something in her mother's tone made Megan turn sharply to stare at her. Again she took note of the carefully coiffed upswept hair that was so rarely attended to these days, of the clean, freshly-pressed dress that her mother had labored over so frantically with the heavy sad iron, of the attentiveness with which she followed the progress of the two men across the street. An attentiveness born perhaps of something stronger than mere friendly concern.

An attentiveness that sprang from precisely the same kind of emotions that were unsettling *her*.

Such realizations strike in an instant, for it seemed that no time at all had passed before Sarah Wheeler realized how she'd spoken to her daughter. She hastened to correct any false impressions her words might have given.

''I'm sorry, Megan,'' she said much too quickly ''I—''

''It's all right.'' Megan sounded small and lost. Hurriedly she turned away, ostensibly to gaze across the street but in reality so that her mother would not be able to see the truth written in her face. A disconcerting, uncomfortable truth, which thus far Megan was the only one to realize.

She and her mother were now rivals.

Both women gazed intently across the street. What they saw was not reassuring. The instant that Josh and the Preacher disappeared inside the Lahood building, the swarm of roughnecks rushed in behind them like so many coyotes closing in on a kill.

Josh Lahood led the Preacher upstairs, away from the dirt and grime of commerce into a rarified realm where the roughnecks were not allowed to follow. They were reduced to milling about the base of the stairway, to mutter expectantly among themselves.

It was quiet upstairs, heavy timber muffling the sounds from the street outside and the warehouse below. The Preacher followed the younger Lahood down a wide hall, then through a door decorated with beaded glass.

Inside, Coy Lahood rose from the chair behind his desk to beam at his guest. He was all conviviality and good humor but for all that he did not extend a welcoming hand. The fact of the matter was, Coy Lahood disliked physical contact. It didn't matter. His visitor was not offended.

"Morning, Reverend! Beautiful day. Beautiful country, this, and a fine place for a man to make his fortune. I'm Coy Lahood."

Unlike the drab exterior of the building, Lahood's sumptuous office might have been transported intact from some substantial San Francisco bank. Dark walnut paneling sealed the walls while a vast Persian carpet blanketed the floor. The desk was fashioned of fine mahogany. Burgundy velvet drapes framed the windows and brass Rochester lamps shone atop the desk.

A few of the roughnecks, unable to stand the suspense, had decided to chance their luck. Now they crowded in behind Josh and the tall stranger, unnaturally subdued in the presence of so much wealth and class. Within the Boss's inner sanctum one spoke only in whispers. They were not much interested in talking anyway. They waited to see what would transpire, hoping they would be permitted to remain.

The Preacher took it all in with a casual glance, then nodded slightly in response to the jovial introduction. "I know."

Lahood had a twinkle in his eye. It had charmed politicians and women, but it was wasted on the Preacher. Lahood had suspected as much, but he was not the man to fail to try every weapon at his disposal, charm included.

"Do you imbibe, Reverend?"

The Preacher smiled at him. "Only after nine in the morning."

He's got a sense of humor. Lahood allowed himself a pleased chuckle. He had expected many things, but not a sense of humor. It was an encouraging sign. Some of the tension that had been building in him prior to the stranger's arrival went away. Could it be he'd been worrying himself over nothing?

Digging in his desk, he produced a bottle and two crystal glasses. He poured two stiff drinks. Uncouth and ignorant of manners, a couple of the roustabouts eyed the golden liquid and licked their lips. Scotch of such quality was as alien to their palates as kind words for the downtrodden. They knew none of their number would ever have the chance to taste of such nectar, but that didn't keep them from dreaming.

Lahood was feeling much better about the forthcoming discussion. As usual, his fool of a boy had exaggerated, just as he was likely to exaggerate any problem he proved incapable of handling.

"When I heard that a parson had arrived in town, I naturally had an image of a pale, scrawny, bible-thumping Easterner complete with linen handkerchief and bad lungs."

"That's me," the Preacher allowed.

Lahood chuckled again. "Hardly." He extended a hand holding a glass, in which reposed six full ounces of the finest Scotch whiskey available anywhere west of the Mississippi. "Your health, sir."

The Preacher took the glass and eyed the contents appreciatively.

Lahood picked up the other glass. "It has occurred to me, sir, that it must be difficult for a man of the faith to carry the message on an empty stomach, so to speak. I take it you have no formal parsonage elsewhere?"

"Mine is a traveling ministry," came the soft reply.

"I see, and a difficult life it must be in this unforgiving country. So I thought to myself; why not invite this devout and humble man to preach right here in town? Why not let this community be his parish? In fact, why not build him a brand new church! We've plenty of sinners hereabouts, Parson. Both local and passing through, with more of 'em coming in every day now that the train stops in Lahood. We've got just about everything we need to make a real town here except a full-time school and a church.

"Think what a permanent church here would mean, Reverend. Families would come to settle down. Hardscrabble miners down on their luck would have a place to turn to. Why, a man like yourself would have so much work to do he'd hardly have a chance to rest." He put on his broadest smile.

"What would you say to taking up your work here, Parson? Full time, in a brand new church of your own design, with a parsonage next door big enough and spacious enough to impress the needy?"

The Preacher continued to regard his own drink, finding something only he could see in the depths of the glass. Lahood hoped it was wisdom. He sipped at his drink, hoping it would inspire his guest to indulge in his own. But the tall man continued to refrain from sampling the liquor as he gazed across the desk at his host.

"I can see how a Preacher could be mighty tempted by an offer like that."

"Indeed. It's a chance for a man of the cloth like yourself to do the work that needs to be done in, shall we say, an appropriate style?"

"Style." The tall man nodded slowly, clearly contemplating Lahood's offer. "Yeah. First thing you know, he'd set his mind on a batch of new clothes. Couldn't go preaching to a real congregation in rags."

"Of course not! Why, we'd have them tailor-made! I know just the tailor in San Francisco. I'm sure he can fashion a frock as fine as he can a gentleman's suit." He pulled back the lapel of his own jacket to display the silk lining. "No reason why a parson shouldn't be comfortable when he's tending to his flock, now is there?"

"Um-humm. Then, of course, he'd get to thinking about the Sunday collection. Even a preacher's got to eat."

"Hell, in a town as rich as Lahood, that preacher'd be a wealthy man! With plenty left over for doing good works, of course. As the leading businessman in the community, I'd make it my personal responsibility to see that the business community's support for the church was appropriate. Distribution of the tithing would be in your hands, naturally." Lahood sipped at his drink, convinced that the bait he'd so stylishly set out was proving irresistible.

The Preacher looked down at his glass again and sighed. "I'm afraid that's why it wouldn't work. Not with me, anyways. As the saying goes, you can't serve God and Mammon both. Might be some preachers who can, but I'm not one of them."

Lahood's eyes narrowed. "Who's this Mammon?" He threw his son a sharp look. "Somebody else setting up a company around here that I haven't heard about?" The younger Lahood shook his head quickly.

"Mammon," the Preacher quietly informed him, "represents money. If you'd read your bible a little more often you'd've known that."

The expression that came over Coy Lahood's face was not pleasant to look upon. All hints of his earlier joviality and friendliness had vanished. He was more than a little upset.

Not only had his kind—no, generous offer—been refused, but he'd been made to appear the fool in the bargain. At the back of the room the roughnecks stirred uneasily, not sure how to react or what to do next. They were confused and nervous.

Nobody stood up to Coy Lahood.

For his part the magnate said nothing, somehow managing to hold his temper. Maybe the first round was finished, but the fight went on. When Lahood got an idea into his head, he clung to it as tenaciously as a pit bull.

So the Preacher wanted to lecture him? All right. He could do a little lecturing of his own. He downed the rest of his drink straight and ostentatiously refilled the glass. The fine Scotch helped to mute his fury. When he addressed his guest again it was with an air of outraged melancholy.

"Let me tell you a thing or two, Reverend. You're new here, and maybe you don't realize how we do things in this part of the world. I opened this country up. When I came in here, there wasn't anything in this part of the Sierras except a few wandering sourdoughs and a lot of grizzlies. Both of 'em are pretty much gone, but not me. I'm still here. I plan to be here for the rest of my life.

"I expect you will be," said the Preacher cryptically. Lahood stared at him for a moment, then went on. He'd told his story many times and never tired of telling it. It flowed from his lips as smoothly as the spiel of any snake-oil salesman.

"I made this town. Hell, when I came here there wasn't any town! The town followed me, not the other way around. You think they call it Lahood because of a lack of imagination? It *deserves* to be called Lahood. The folks who live in this county, they know who's responsible for it, and for the post office being here, and the train depot, and all the other civilized services they've gotten used to." He walked over to the window and gazed out over his fiefdom.

"I brought jobs here, and industry. The sawmill on Adams Creek makes a profit because of the lumber I buy. Blankenship is here because there are enough permanent residents in the area now to support another store besides mine. I've built an empire here with my own two hands, and I never asked for anyone's help. All I ever asked for was a fair chance to build. And ain't nobody taking what I've sweated and bled for away from me the way they ruined John Sutter."

"Sounds reasonable enough," said the Preacher understandingly. "What's that got to do with the folks up in Carbon Canyon?"

"Those squatters, Reverend, lie around there and play at gold-mining with their pans and Long Toms. Toys! Mining's changed from the days when a man could stake himself a claim and get rich with a pick and shovel. It's a business now, a big business. Companies moving in from back East with their engineers and geologists and their fancy consultants. Me, I hire local folks, miners who can't make it anymore on their own and men who don't belong in a store. I provide jobs for ten times as many men as are scrabbling through the dirt up in Carbon." He turned from the window, put both hands on his desk, and leaned forward.

"Times are changing, Preacher. Those squatters are standing in the way of progress."

"Whose progress?" was the even reply. "Yours—or theirs?"

The older man shook his head sadly. "You aren't listening to me, Parson. Haven't you heard a word I've said?"

"I heard. What you say about the big companies moving in makes sense, but that doesn't make it right. I know that a man's got a right to the kind of life he chooses for himself, and if that means he wants to pan for gold and be the poorer for it, that's his choice. That's a lot of what this country's all about. Maybe he'll end up poorer in the pocket, but not in spirit."

Lahood's lips tightened. Reaching into an inside coat pocket, he removed an official-looking document and tossed it on the desk.

"It doesn't matter anyway. I'm trying to be fair with you, Reverend, but I don't have to be. Look at that! That's a writ. Comes straight from Sacramento. I didn't leave my business here for three weeks because I needed a vacation. I know a lot of the right people to know in this state, Reverend. I like them, and they like me.'' He nodded at the sheaf of papers. ''That tells me I've got mineral rights to the whole damn canyon!''

Except for a single brief glance the Preacher ignored the document. It teetered for a moment on the edge of the desk and then wafted to the floor.

''Hardly seems likely. If you really had those rights, you'd have started exercising them long before now.''

''Now how could I do that? I just got back.''

The Preacher shook his head slowly. ''You're an impatient man, Lahood. You've got telegraph wires running to the depot. You would've wired through to your son as soon as you had the proper signatures on any writ and you'd be working Carbon Creek right now. The fact that you aren't tells me that you know that you can't. Those folks have legally registered claims. You can't touch the canyon unless they resign them or abandon their sites.''

''Damn it,'' Lahood raged, ''pick up that writ. Read it!''

If anything, the Preacher's voice grew softer as he replied. ''If it was worth the paper it's printed on you wouldn't have tried to bribe me first. Maybe Lahood, California, is in need of a church, but you're not, and you wouldn't have been in such a hurry to build one if your writ was legal.''

The two men locked eyes for a moment longer. Then Lahood slumped back into his chair. He shoved his newly refilled glass aside. His bluff had been called. The game was over.

The first game. The polite one.

When he spoke again his voice had a different quality, of curiosity and detachment. It was as though he was continuing the conversation solely for appearance's sake, as if he'd already made the necessary decisions. He was still talking, but he was no longer listening.

"You puzzle me, Reverend. Yes you do. Tell me, what's your business with those tin-pans?"

"No business. Leastwise, not the kind you mean. They're my friends. That's all there is to it."

"Is there? Well, no matter. I've tried to be square with you, Reverend. I've done my best to play straight, and you've thrown it back in my face. There are some who might call that kind of an attitude un-Christian. But I still remember my manners, and I like to show I can be reasonable even when I've been treated badly.

"So I'm giving you and your 'friends' twenty-four hours to pack up and leave, or my men'll ride through the canyon and *run* you out. I've been a law-abiding man up 'til now. Hasn't been easy, either, when you consider the appetites of some of the critters I'm forced to hire for want of better material.

"But time is precious and I'm not getting any younger. Those squatters have worn out my patience, Reverend. Any blood gets spilt will be on your hands. If they're your friends, you'll tell 'em to get out before somebody gets hurt."

The stranger's eyes narrowed. He didn't reply, just stared at the mining magnate as he'd once stared at his spoiled, imperious offspring not so very long ago. Whatever there was in that stare gave even a man like Coy Lahood reason to pause.

"You're a troublemaker, stranger," he finally declared softly. "You spell Bad Ass in letters that stretch from here to Seattle. We don't want your kind hanging around our town."

The Preacher still held the glass of golden liquor in one hand. Now he knocked back half the contents in a single swallow, smacked his lips, then downed the remainder with equal swiftness and precision. Carefully he placed the fine Austrian crystal back on the burnished surface of the desk.

"Thanks for the drink." Turning on his heel, he moved purposefully toward the door. The roughnecks made way for him like jackels leaving a path for a lion.

"Preacher," Lahood snapped. The tall stranger halted and glanced back. His expression had not changed. "I've reasoned with you and I've bargained with you and both times I've come up short. But what's mine is mine, and if you make me fight for it, I will." He hesitated, then continued as though lecturing a particularly bright but exceedingly stubborn child.

"I didn't want to have to say this, but you've forced me to it. You and those damn dumb tin-pans. There's a man—a U.S. Marshal. He keeps the peace, if you take my meaning. Some folks say his methods are . . . unorthodox. But we're a long ways from Washington out here, and sometimes men choose not to work by the book. His name is Stockburn, and he won't be as patient as me."

A heavy silence hung over the office. To a few of Lahood's more widely traveled hooligans the name Stockburn had meaning. To the rest it did not, though they were bursting to ask their more knowledgeable colleagues about it. But no one dared speak.

Until the Preacher, in a tone different from any he'd employed thus far, asked quietly, "Those people in Carbon Canyon: would you be willing to offer them cash for their claims? Buy them out fair and legal?"

Trying hard not to show his surprise at this sudden turnabout and sensing he'd somehow gained the upper hand, Lahood gestured expansively. "Why, I'd do anything to avoid bloodshed. You think it pleases me to talk about building a church one minute and riding down squatters the next?'' Aware he might be overdoing the false piety just a trifle, he hastened to add, ''How about one hundred dollars a head?''

''I said legal *and* fair. How about a thousand?''

Lahood couldn't contain himself. He burst out laughing. Taking their Boss's cue; the cluster of roughnecks joined in the outburst of unexpected hilarity.

Wiping the tears from his eyes, Lahood finally regained control of himself. ''Tell you what I'll do,'' he replied condescendingly. ''I'll come up to a hundred twenty-five. That's more money than most of those tin-pans will see in a year, and they don't have to do a lick of work for it. All they have to do is walk out.''

The Preacher's eyes bored into him. ''Stockburn—and his 'deputies'—will cost you a lot more than that.''

The humor drained instantly from Lahood's face, to be replaced by a look of total surprise. His voice was hushed and he gaped at the Preacher in disbelief.

''Now, how would *you* know that?''

His guest ignored the query. ''How much is a clear conscience worth to you, Lahood?''

Behind the two men Josh, McGill, and the others exchanged confused whispers. Something had changed. The atmosphere in the office was different somehow, and they did not understand the reason for the change. The elder Lahood and the Preacher possessed a piece of knowledge that was denied to everyone else.

The whispers were fading by the time Lahood spoke again, his voice flat and unemotional. ''A thousand dollars per claim, then. For all of 'em or none. I can't mine properly unless I can work the whole canyon.''

Murmurs of disbelief ran through the assembled roughnecks. Any talk of amounts of more than three figures was beyond their comprehension.

"But I want them all out of there in twenty-four hours," Lahood growled, "or the deal's off."

The Preacher nodded his understanding. "I'll tell them." He turned and strode through the door. For an instant his footsteps could be heard in the hall beyond, then on the stairway, and then they too had disappeared.

At which point Josh Lahood and McGill rushed the desk, voicing their disbelief and giving vent at last to their pent-up curiosity.

"A thousand a claim! Papa, have you lost your mind?"

"Hell, Mr. Lahood, sir," said an incredulous McGill, "me and the boys would've chased them dirt-scrabblers all the way to the Mexican border for half that!"

"Would you now?" replied Lahood quietly. "It's done."

"But Papa—a thousand dollars a claim!" Josh still couldn't believe it. "There must be thirty or forty families up there."

"I said it's *done*." Lahood stared at his son until the younger man retreated. "I know what I'm doing, boy. McGill, you tend to your mining and leave the confrontations to me."

"Yes, boss," said the subdued foreman.

"In twenty-four hours I want the monitor and its support team ready to move. I want to be washing gravel in Carbon by the end of the week. Then we'll see who's lost his mind." He glared up at his son, who looked abashed if not convinced.

"Now get out. All of you. I've got work to do and so do the rest of you. Those of you who still like your jobs, that is." The room cleared instantly, Josh retreating more slowly than the rest and pausing just long enough to cast a last querulous glance in his father's direction.

Alone among the fruits of his labors, Lahood sat and

pondered the conversation with the peculiar Preacher. It hadn't gone quite as he'd expected, or as he'd hoped, but he could live with the outcome. An intriguing individual, that Preacher. Intriguing and puzzling. He sighed, then reached for his pen and blank paper.

If only so many of the fools weren't on his side.

Hull couldn't see the buckboard clearly as he emerged from Blankenship's because his arms were piled high with goods.

". . . Paid off both accounts in full, Sarah," he was saying as he picked his way down the steps, "and had enough left over to pay up Spider's! He'll pay me back when he can. He's a funny old coot but he's honest.

"You should've been in there to see Blankenship's face." He stepped off the last step onto the street. "He couldn't believe it when I showed him the nugget. Had to weigh it out three times, and he still wanted to melt it down to make sure I hadn't gone and wrapped some gold around a lead ingot, but he finally—" He broke off in midsentence when he saw that both women were sitting rigidly upright in the back of the wagon and staring across the street.

Of their protector there was no sign.

"Where is he?" Hull asked sharply.

"In there. Josh Lahood came and asked him to go with him and they went in there." Sarah nodded at the Lahood building.

Hull took a deep breath, then carefully deposited the supplies in the rear of the wagon—except for the brand-new axe handle. This he hefted in both hands as he came back around to the front of the wagon. What he'd do once inside the warehouse he didn't know for sure, only that it was incumbent on him to do *something*.

As it turned out, events saved him from himself.

Clint Eastwood is the nameless stranger who mysteriously appears in the Warner Brothers film 'PALE RIDER.'

Coy Lahood (Left: Richard Dysart) with his son Josh (Christopher Penn) plan to use Club (Richard Kiel) to drive the miners from Carbon Canyon.

Megan Wheeler (Sydney Penney) prays for her dog and for a savior from the Lahoods' terrorizing.

Hull Barret (Michael Moriarty) and Sarah (Carrie Snodgrass), Megan's mother, after the latest ransacking of the Carbon Creek mining community by Lahood's men.

The nameless stranger arrives in town.

Josh forces himself on Megan (above), while in town his father's hired guns riddle a miner with bullets (below).

The stranger puts an end to Josh's attempts (above) and takes Megan home to safety (below).

Once Megan is safe, the stranger sets out to rid Carbon Canyon of Lahood and his men once and for all.

"Look," Megan whispered, "they're coming out."

Sure enough, the porch was filling up with Lahood's men as they slowly filed out the front door. Hull hitched up his jeans and started toward them, utterly terrified but equally unwilling to abandon his newfound friend, no matter how foolish it had been of him to go with Josh Lahood. Maybe if he raised enough of a ruckus it would . . .

He stopped. The Preacher appeared, pushing easily past the roughnecks. He started to cross the street. No one moved to challenge him. As soon as he saw Hull advancing to meet him he raised a hand in a reassuring wave. Rescued from his own bravery, the miner let the axe handle drop to his side. Behind him Sarah sagged visibly with relief while Megan could barely suppress a triumphant smile.

The two men met in the middle of the street, and Hull joined the Preacher in walking back to the wagon.

"What were you doing in there?" Hull didn't try to hide the concern in his voice. "You might never have come out."

"Unlikely," the Preacher told him calmly. "Lahood invited me in for a drink." He glanced down at the axe handle dangling from the miner's hand and smiled. "Thanks for the thought."

Hull looked from his companion back to the Lahood building. "You were in there all the time I was in Blankenship's?"

"Yep. Lahood and I, we had us a talk."

"About what?" Hull asked curiously.

They had almost reached the buckboard. "It concerns everyone working in the canyon, not just me and you and the Wheelers. Best thing to do is tell everyone about it at the same time. Tonight."

"If you think that's best, Preacher, then it's all right with me. But don't expect me to take it easy on the ride back."

The tall man just grinned.

VII

The bonfire fed on summer-dried juniper. It pushed back the chill of the Sierra night and illuminated the faces of the men who sat or stood on its perimeter. Young and old, they represented all the families who had chosen to settle in the canyon as well as those solitary men who sought similar riches there.

At the moment they were silent, listening intently to the stranger who'd appeared so suddenly among them. Only when he'd concluded his talk, which primarily involved the conveying of Lahood's buy-out offer to them, was there a rush of hands skyward.

"Aye—aye!" The chorus of affirmation rang out around the circle. Hull Barret performed a quick count.

"All those opposed," he asked when he'd totaled the number of upthrust hands.

"*Me*, dang it!" The solitary voice was touched by time but still rang out clear and unmistakeable.

Everyone turned to face the man who'd sung out against the majority. Rising from where he'd been sitting, Spider Conway moved closer to the fire so that his neighbors could see him clearly. He tried to sting every one of them with his eyes. Hull watched him too, as did the Preacher, who sat on a nearby log.

"Aw, come on, Spider, it's gettin' late!" one man said tiredly.

"Yeah, we've already taken the vote," said another.

"I'll have my say! I was here first and, by the looks of it, I may be here last, but I'm entitled to tell you what I think about this business and you're all damn well obligated to listen." A few groans greeted this declaration, along with the admonitions of those who felt it only fair to listen with an open mind to whatever the canyon's oldest resident might have to say.

Conway turned a slow circle as he spoke, trying to impress his feelings as well as his argument on every man there.

"Me and Coy Lahood seen a lot o' ground together, startin' back in '55. I probably know as much about how his mind works as any man alive, including that fool boy o' his, and there's one thing I can tell you for sure about this business of buyin' all of us out: greedy Coy Lahood may be, but he ain't no fool."

"We all know that," said Everson boredly. "Get to the point, Spider. If you've got one."

The old miner gazed sharply at the man who'd spoken. "It's the point you want, is it? All right. You just think on this: if Coy Lahood's willin' to cough up a thousand dollars a claim, including for those that ain't give up more'n an ounce or two o' dust, you can be damn sure he ain't doin' it out of the goodness of his heart. He couldn't be, 'cause there ain't no goodness *in* Coy Lahood's heart! The only way he'd come to part with that much money is if he knows that each claim's worth five or ten times as much as he's payin' us for 'em!"

It was clear from their reactions that this thought had not

occurred to any of the other miners. A murmur ran around the circle, and a few men began to voice their agreement. You didn't have to like Spider Conway (and for assorted reasons some of the men did not) to appreciate his logic. What he said about Lahood and his motives made sense.

Then Jake Henderson spoke up. "I ain't going to argue with you on what you've said, Spider. The way Lahood works, maybe each claim *is* worth more than a thousand.

"But the way we work, we're lucky to see a thousand dollars in a year. Some of us ain't never seen that much money, least of all at one time." He spat into the sand. "Me, I'm plumb tuckered out. My hands are wore to the bone from swinging a shovel. Me and the woman are tired of freezing through every winter without any meat on the table but what I can kill. I ain't none too keen on sittin' out another one. I say we take the offer. There's always the chance to move on, maybe up north Oregon ways, and strike it rich on another claim. One where a bunch of cutthroats don't come riding down on you once a week."

There was plenty of support around the fire for Henderson's way of thinking, but Conway refused to give in.

"First off, you know as well as I, Jake, that all the easy placer claims were panned out or bought up years ago. The only gold that's left in this country is stuff that's harder to get at, up here in the rocks. As for up Oregon way, way I hear tell it that country's good for fishin', farmin', and loggin' trees, but there ain't enough gold up there to fill a tooth." He spat into the fire. The wind bore away the hiss.

"You ain't lookin' at your own claim straight. What about that nugget Hull here washed out this morning?"

"Freak luck," Henderson snapped. "You've been mining

right next to him for more'n two years and you ain't made a strike like that.''

"Thanks for remindin' me," Spider replied. A couple of the men chuckled. "I keep tellin' you." He turned a slow circle. "I keep tellin' all of you that the real gold's here, just like Barret found. It's just down under the top gravel is all, and you got to pan that or sluice that away to get at the pay dirt."

"Pay dirt my ass," grumbled an unseen speaker.

"All right then, tell me this," Conway said, trying another track, "suppose one of you struck a thousand bucks in nuggets? Would you cash in your claim, quit your diggin's and blow town? Or would you keep diggin' for some more?''

The miners set to arguing among themselves. A few were ready to leave immediately, like Henderson, while the majority considered all the work and hope, all the long days and endless dreams they'd already poured into their claims. But even to the latter group, Lahood's offer was tempting. A thousand dollars in the hand was a tough nut to turn down when all you had to use for a counterweight was hope.

Spider listened hard to the conversations, trying to determine which way the wind was blowing. Then he had a new thought and spun to peer down at the tall man who'd come among them.

"You've heard what I've had to say and what the others have had to say, Preacher. What do you think we ought to do?" Other voices took up the query in a rush.

The man with the collar sat on his log and considered. Finally he looked up at them, first at Conway, then Henderson, and then the rest.

"What I think doesn't count. It's your sweat he's buying.

My life isn't here. I don't lay claim to one foot of this canyon, and so I can't have any say in the business.''

This reply was not the one the miners wanted to hear. They didn't want honesty from the stranger. They wanted him to make the decision they themselves were unable to make. They wanted him to give them The Answer.

He listened to their expostulations. ''Maybe you all should sleep on it, decide in the morning. Doesn't pay a man to be hasty with his future.''

Some of the men were willing to accept this advice, but not the tenacious Conway. ''What if we can't decide in the morning?'' He gestured toward his vacillating neighbors. ''We ain't havin' much luck makin' any decisions now. I don't see that a night's sleep is goin' to make much difference. We could argue on it from now 'til doomsday without reachin' a consensus, and we ain't got 'til doomsday.''

''No, you don't,'' the Preacher agreed quietly.

''What happens if we take your advice and we do wait until morning and we still can't decide? What then?''

The Preacher was using a piece of driftwood to trace a pattern in the sand in front of him. No one thought to look at it. They were all watching his face, waiting expectantly for him to tell them what to do.

''I expect,'' he finally said, ''that Lahood would take that as the same as saying 'no.' ''

''And then what? More riders?'' Ev Gossage wanted to know.

The Preacher hesitated a moment before replying. ''Something more than that, I'm afraid. He said he'd call in a U.S. Marshal.''

Hull Barret frowned. ''Is that supposed to frighten us? Hell, I wish he would bring some real law down here. What kind of threat is that? We don't have anything to fear from the law."

"You don't understand." The Preacher looked up at his friend. "There's the law as it's written. That's the kind of law that's represented by your claims. Then there's the law that some men know how to twist to suit their own ends. That's Lahood's kind of law. And the poorer you are, and the farther away from any other kind of law, the more twisted it can become and the easier it is to twist. This man Lahood's talking about bringing in isn't just any Marshal."

There was something in the Preacher's tone that subdued even the bellicose Spider Conway. "What are you gettin' at, Preacher? What kind of Marshal is Lahood talkin' about?"

"His name's Stockburn, but that doesn't tell a man much. You have to know more than his name to know what kind of man he is. I don't know how he ever managed to get himself appointed Marshal, but that doesn't matter. Not everything that happens on Earth happens for the good. Fact remains that he is what he is. 'There are more things in Heaven and Earth, Horatio, than are dreamt of in your philosophy.'"

Conway made a quick scan of the solemn circle of miners. "Ain't nobody here named Horatio, Preacher. Ain't never been."

The tall man did not smile. "There's more than just the Marshal. Stockburn's got six deputies been with him a long time. Six—and they'll uphold whatever law pays them the most. Killing's their way of life." He paused to study their faces. "I want you all to know that, because unless you accept Lahood's offer, it's likely you'll be meeting up with them."

Until the Preacher's short speech the miners had only been

uncertain and confused. Now a new element had been introduced into the equation they were attempting to resolve: fear.

Spider Conway was as puzzled as any of them. The words the Preacher had spoken weren't the ones the old sourdough had been prepared to hear. He stared at the tall man.

"You talk like there's no doubt in your mind about this fella. You know this Stockburn?"

"I've heard of him," was the soft reply.

It was dead quiet around the fire. Then Hull Barret stepped out of the circle. "All right, now we know what we're up against. Me, I think it stinks. Lahood ain't just sayin' 'take my offer.' He's sayin' 'take my offer or else.' It's one thing to offer to buy a man out, but rubbin' his face in it ain't right."

A chorus of protests rose from the anxious men. "We're family men, Hull," said one.

"Yeah," another added, "we ain't no match for seven guns!"

"Bullshit!" Hull glared at them. Silhouetted by the flickering light of the fire, he appeared somehow changed from the soft-spoken, easy-going man so well known to his neighbors. There was a new confidence in his voice, an unexpected assertiveness to his manner.

"How many of us are there? Twenty! I heard the Preacher same as the rest of you. I know these men he's talking about are—professionals. But I fought at Bull Run and Shiloh. Henderson, what about you? You going to let some Marshal scare you off your land? You were at Manassas." Jake Henderson nodded slowly in agreement.

"And Ev—Ev, you were with Farragut at Mobile." Ev Gossage looked away but didn't deny it. "You ran torpedoes—you goin' to run away from half a dozen hired pistols?" He turned a slow circle. "It's still twenty against one, ain't it?

And we know how to pull a damn trigger, don't we? You all fought for Jackson and Grant and Lee. Now's the time to fight for yourselves and your kin."

"That was years ago, Hull," said Ev Gossage quietly. "I didn't have a wife and kids with me then, and Grant ain't here to tell us what to do, and there's no cavalry or cannon to back us up."

"Didn't have no cannon with us at Vicksburg," muttered another of the men. "Fought our way through the damn swamps, we did."

There was a flurry of agreement from a majority of the others. The War Between the States had taught most of them how to use a gun. Sure they were older now, with families some of 'em, but that was a skill never forgotten once learned.

On the other hand, they'd been common foot soldiers. This Stockburn and his men were professionals.

Ev Gossage raised a hand for quiet. "If it comes down to it, I'm willin' as any man to fight before I'll be driven off my claim. You're right about that, Hull. We shouldn't let ourselves be run off. But dammit, we're not talking about being run off! Lahood's offer is fair, and I ain't just got myself to think about. There's the missus and the kids depending on me. They weren't in the war and they can't fight back. If I decide to go and get myself killed, that's my decision, but I got to think of them. I still vote we take the money and use it to start over fresh somewheres else."

Gossage's reasoning provoked a new storm of controversy. Hull had to shout to make himself heard.

"Hey, startin' fresh always sounds good when folks get in trouble. That's why most of us are here now instead of grubbin' out on somebody else's farm or clerkin' in somebody else's store back east. But before we vote to pack it in, we ought to ask ourselves what we're all about, what we're doin' here in the first place. 'Cause if it's no more'n money, well then, hell, we're no better than Lahood himself.'' He waited a moment for the import of his words to sink in.

"So you all look at yourselves and then tell me: why *did* we all of us come out here and set ourselves down in this godforsaken—excuse me, Preacher—place?"

Spider Conway took a seat close to the fire and tossed another split length of juniper on the blaze. Sparks flew, disappeared into the night sky. He was nearing the age when the cold started to dig its way into a man's bones, making him ache when he had to get up early in the morning or slip out of a warm bed to stir the fire in the pot-bellied stove. But the chill was still a long ways from reaching his heart.

Hull gestured toward him. "Spider here asked us a question. If one of us turned up a thousand dollars' worth of nuggets, would he quit? Hell, no! He'd build his family a better house, buy his kids some new clothes. Maybe even," and here he glanced ever so briefly in the Preacher's direction, "build a school or a church. If we were farmers we'd be plantin' crops. If we raised cattle we'd be tendin' 'em. But we're miners, so we pan and dig and break our backs for gold. But hell, gold ain't what we're *about*."

They listened silently; Gossage and Henderson and Williams and the rest of them, conscious that Barret, who was one of their own, was on to something all the talk and arguing had so far avoided.

"This canyon's our home," Hull went on. "Our dream. We came out here to find gold, sure, but also to put down roots. To raise our families. God knows it ain't much, but it's a start. Better than any of us would've had back east, or we wouldn't be here now.

"We've buried relations in this ground. This was their dream, too. Some of 'em died for it. Are we gonna take a thousand dollars and leave their graves untended? Don't we owe 'em more than that? We owe ourselves more'n that. If we sell out here, what price do we put on our dignity the next time? Two thousand? Less? Or just the best offer?

"One thing you can be damn sure of. If Ev's right and there is another good place, sooner or later another Lahood's goin' to find it too, and then what'll we do? I say we make our stand against the Lahoods of the world here and now!"

There was utter silence around the campfire. Normally a reticent type, Hull was suddenly embarrassed at having made himself the center of attention. Having done so, however, there was no place to hide.

Besides, the words had to be said, and it had been left to him to say them.

It was Spider Conway who jumped to his feet to stand next to him in the spotlight.

"I say to hell with Lahood!" He raked over his fellow miners with his eyes. Most of them were younger and stronger than the old sourdough. They knew it and so did he, and it embarrassed them. The old man knew exactly what he was doing. If he couldn't argue them into fighting, then maybe with the aid of Barret's unexpectedly eloquent soliloquy he could shame them into sticking up for their rights.

Hull was as surprised as anyone when Ev Gossage stepped forward to join them. "I, uh, I ain't a brave man, but I ain't no coward, neither. I didn't run from Pickett, and I sure as hell ain't gonna run from the likes of Coy Lahood. We took our chances this far. I think it's been worth it and I'd hate to chuck it all just now." He gazed out into the darkness, past his friends and neighbors, past the places weakly lit by the fire.

"I been thinking about what Hull just said. The family and me, we been here over a year now, and I kind of like this canyon. We've seen what Lahood's methods do to the land. I'd hate to see that happen here in Carbon. See, way I figure it, we owe this canyon something. It's been decent enough to us, and I reckon we ought to be square by it. That means not givin' it over to a man like Lahood.

"So—I vote we keep it up. Hull's right. There's more at stake here than gold, and a lot more that's worth fightin' for."

"Hell with Coy Lahood's money!" shouted Williams. "I ain't leavin' Carbon until I'm good and ready."

The slight youth seated next to Williams sprang to his feet and glared excitedly around the circle. As the youngest unmarried miner in the canyon, Peterson was hardly older than Megan and had kept his peace in front of his elders. He could do so no longer.

"I ain't givin' up my home! First I ever had and I'm damned if I'm gonna be run out of it!"

"T'hell with Lahood and his gunnies!" The cry was taken up by each man in turn as the men found themselves caught up in a whirlwind of unexpected commitment.

"Yeah . . . I got a rifle! . . . let 'em come! . . . We'll blow him and his dogs back to Sacramento!"

Overwhelmed by their newly resurgent enthusiasm and the spirit of defiance, they fairly danced around the fire. Only one man remained seated. The Preacher sat on his log and watched them, his eyes flicking from one celebrant to another. Now that they'd made their decision, they were trying to dance the tension away.

It would take a lot more than enthusiasm to stop Stockburn and his deputies, the Preacher knew. As he watched them gambol and prance around the flames, his eyes were filled with understanding and concern—and something else.

Sadness.

Because he knew what was coming now, knew it as surely as these simple but good folk did not. Just as he knew what he was going to have to do to prevent it.

No one paid much attention to him as he rose, turned, and walked away from the circle of men who continued to shout their defiance at the stars. Their yelling and whooping quickly faded behind him, as did the tiny pyramid of light that was their fire. He needed neither lamp nor torch. There was enough of a moon to show him the way.

He climbed without any particular destination in mind, following the only trail that wound upward. Knowing what he knew, he could not join in the celebration that was taking place below, and he did not wish to dampen it with any more truthful answers to difficult questions. Better to leave them to their newfound assurance and confidence.

They were going to need all of it they could muster.

It was good to be alone on that cool, clear evening. Except that he wasn't truly alone. There was the forest to keep him company, and the night sounds of small mammals skittering through the roots and bushes. He had the companionship of the patient moon and a few curious clouds. Somewhere a Great Horned Owl soared just above the tops of the pines, its huge yellow eyes scanning the earth below, intent on small murders. A fox's eyes glittered with moonlight as it froze to follow the movements of the tall human. It waited like a brown sculpture between two ironwood bushes until the man had gone and only his scent remained, and then continued about its business.

Only to find itself confronted by the same figure. The fox, which had thought itself well concealed, was not used to being surprised in its woods. It found itself petrified by that unexpectedly direct stare. Then it bolted for the deeper forest.

The Preacher smiled and walked on.

Eventually he found himself in a small glade, the grass surrounded by towering sugar pines. His appearance suggested a man asleep on his feet. Actually he was as alert as ever. His mind was doing all the work while his body rested. He was as motionless as one of the rough-barked trees that surrounded him.

A pine cone slid over a rock; a tiny sound. There were only two in that part of the forest with hearing sharp enough to detect it, and the fox had fled. Turning, the Preacher discovered that he had been followed.

The feminine shape was backlit by the moon. Having tensed at the sound, he now let himself relax. He would not have been surprised if Barret had come looking for him to make sure he was all right. He would not have been surprised if one of the miners had sought to kill him and so collect a reward from Lahood. But surprised he was when he was able to identify this unexpected shadow.

She wore her hair up in a graceful sweeping curve, and for an instant he was certain it was Sarah Wheeler. Then as the figure came close he saw that he was only half right.

The woman paused ten feet away and pointed to the base of the largest tree in the glade. A tiny white cross marked a place between two gnarled roots. The Preacher would not have noticed the marker if it hadn't been pointed out to him.

"I buried my dog over there," Megan told him slowly.

He responded with a reassuring smile. "That makes it hallowed ground then, doesn't it?"

She hesitated until she was sure he wasn't teasing her, then came toward him. "I said a prayer for him. He was a good dog, never bothered anyone." In the moonlight her eyes were glistening. "It says in the bible that animals don't go to heaven. I don't think I want to go if there aren't any animals there."

"There are all kinds of ways to interpret what the bible says. I think if your dog was a good one, you'll find him there one day. What happened to him?"

Her tone darkened. "Lahood's men killed him. They didn't have to do that. He wasn't big enough to hurt them. They shot him for fun. Why would anyone do a thing like that, Preacher?"

He sighed and stared through the trees toward the far ridge. "Some men forget that they're a part of the Earth. They think they're above it. When they learn otherwise it's generally too late for them. When did it happen?"

"During the last raid. It was after the raid that I prayed. I prayed for a miracle."

His gaze dropped to her again. "Well, maybe some day you'll get what you asked for. Miracles are mighty unpredictable things. It's the folks that spend all their time looking for them that never seem to find 'em. I always say it's better to get on with your life as best you can without hoping for a miracle to get you out of trouble."

"That was the day you arrived."

The Preacher's smile widened and he allowed himself a

small chuckle. Megan could feel herself blushing, and she averted her eyes from his face. Somehow she got the words out.

"There's something else."

"What might that be, Megan."

"I think I love you."

This revelation did not surprise him. "Nothing wrong with that. If there was more love in the world, there'd be a lot less dying. Some folks have a hard time understanding that."

"Then, if there's nothing wrong with being in love, there can't be anything wrong with *making* love, either."

That gave him pause. He considered his reply very carefully. "I think it's better to practice just loving for awhile before you start the other. Lots of people don't understand that, and they end up feeling awfully confused when things don't work out the way they're supposed to. They don't understand why they're so confused, and then they get hurt. It ain't quite as simple as it seems."

"Then if I practice just loving for awhile, would you— teach me about the other?"

"Most folks don't usually get around to that until after they're married."

"But I'll be sixteen next month. Mama was sixteen when she was married. Will you teach me then?"

The Preacher drew in a long breath, turned his face back to the trees. "I won't be here next month."

Megan's lower jaw dropped. "What?"

He tried to be as gentle as possible. "It's the way it has to be, Megan. I'll be leaving soon."

She took a step backward, shaking her head disbelievingly as her eyes began to fill with tears. They spilled down her girlish cheeks, bright in the moonlight.

"But you can't. I—I don't want you to!"

"I don't want to, either. It's just the way it is. You've got to understand that, Megan. There are times when we can't control what we've got to do, even if it goes against what we'd like. That's part of growing up."

Sobbing, she threw her arms around him and held on tight. "You can't!"

He smiled down at her. She was lost next to his massive form. "Hey, now. This is no way to pass the test."

Megan's reply was barely audible. "What test?"

"You mean I never told you about the test?" She shook her head. He held her gently as he spoke. "If you love something, set it free. If it comes back to you, it's yours. If it doesn't, then it never was. There are many ways to test what love is, and that's the best one I've found." Disengaging himself, he peered down into her upturned face.

"As you get older you'll find there'll be many things you love that you'll have to set free. You won't want to do it because it'll always hurt, no matter how you try to convince yourself otherwise. But sometimes it's the greatest test that your love is real. It's not an easy thing to do, but it's important for you to be able to do it."

"But I don't want to let you go! I want you to be with me forever."

"I understand. But you must believe me, Megan. It wasn't meant to be. No matter how badly we want them there are some things in life that just can't be ours. It may hurt a lot now, but I promise you that it will go away, and one of these days the right man will come along. Then none of this will matter anymore. I promise you that.

"You say that you want me to teach you about love. Well, I'm teaching you something now, and like a lot of lessons you'll be learning, I'm afraid that this is one you're not going to like very much no matter how I try to teach it to you." He smiled wider and looked past her, through the trees.

"Now, if I was your mama, right about this time I'd be starting to worry where you'd got to."

He bent low to plant an avuncular kiss on her forehead. It wasn't at all what she wanted, what she'd followed him to the glade to find, and it made her angrier than nothing at all. The worst part of it was she didn't know why she was so angry.

Then a new thought exploded in her mind with all the brilliance of a Fourth-of-July skyrocket, and she was sure she knew why it had all gone so wrong. She started backing away from him.

"I know why you're doing this. I know why you're saying these things to me. It's because of my mama. She's the one you love, isn't it?"

The Preacher's reply was kindly without being condescending. "Your mama's a fine woman—and so are you."

"The way you look at her." Megan's frustration found an outlet in an excuse instead of in understanding. "The way she looks at you. It's true! Well I don't care!"

Sighing, the tall man knew there was little he could say that hadn't already been said. "Megan—"

"You can have her!" She was screaming as she backed away from him now. "I never want to see you again, ever! I hope you go to hell! I hope you die!"

He opened his mouth to try and calm her, but she was already gone, a flash of tears and gingham skirts in the moonlight. Another man might have run after her, worried, but the Preacher knew better than to do that. She was not old enough to understand such a gesture, and too old not to be hurt further by the reason behind it. So he just stood there, sad and immobile in the center of the glade, until he was certain she was gone.

Then he resumed his solitary stroll.

VIII

The sun had yet to clear the eastern ramparts of the High Sierra when the Preacher rode into Cobalt Canyon. The thunder of the monitor drew his attention to the scarred upper slopes of the narrow defile. A few forlorn scrub bushes and weeds still clung to the barren, blasted slopes where the powerful jet of water had not quite chewed away every fragment of topsoil. He paused long enough to study the moonscape for a moment, then urged his mount onward.

The monitor crew moved the water cannon slowly. Trees bent, then toppled into the creek as the earth beneath them was gouged away. Spray surrounded the men with mist and rainbows, softening their appearance if not the grim work they were doing.

Watching the crew at its work, the Preacher's expression grew dark. No one seemed to have a care for the havoc they were wreaking. They were as mindless as the machine they operated.

He was not against mining, not even against organized, large-scale company-run mining. But the use of the water cannon was inexcusable. It was worse than a forest fire, because it left nothing behind to regenerate the soil. It swept the country cleaner than a tornado.

Why, the Devil himself could not have devised a more thorough instrument of destruction.

Josh Lahood was one of those directing the awesome stream of water. He could have left the arduous duty to someone else, but he took his turn behind the monitor to impress his father. It was hard, painful work, and he and the man who was working alongside him were glad when the time came to relinquish control of the nozzle to Club.

As he strode clear of the spray, wiping at his damp face and flexing his arms to ease the strain in tired muscles, he caught sight of a horseman where there shouldn't have been one. Then he recognized the tall figure seated on the well-worn saddle, and his hand slipped automatically toward his gun. The fingers hovered above the handle, then slowly retreated when it became apparent that the intruder had no intention of stopping to confront him.

The stranger did, however, turn long enough to glance casually in Josh's direction. He had to raise his voice in order to make himself heard above the monitor's roar. The message he'd come to deliver was as brief as it was meaningful.

"Tell your father they turned him down!"

The younger Lahood glared sullenly at the horseman as he wheeled his horse about and trotted back the way he'd come. Then Josh spat once at the already sodden earth, turned, and shouted.

"McGill!"

The train whistle split the afternoon air as the engine slowed to a halt next to the depot. Up near the locomotive the engineer and his assistant fumbled with the spout set into the base of the big water tank. Steam hissed and boiled as some of the water spilled from the leaky iron pipe to strike hot iron.

The stationmaster emerged from his shack, stretched, and

scratched at his beard as he waited for the door to the mailcar to open. Unseen hands slid it aside. The trainman tossed out a small sack of mail.

"More'n usual today, Whitey."

"Yep." The stationmaster bent to retrieve the sack. "Gettin' downright crowded hereabouts. Two stores, a barber—next thing you know some fool'll want to be pavin' the street. Why, it's almost like civilization."

"Might not be as bad as it sounds. Me, I've been to Frisco and I like the way civilization looks. She's got a neat figure."

Whitey grinned. "That ain't civilization. That's bathing."

The trainman sniffed ostentatiously. "Whatever you want to call it, you could use a little civilizin', Whitey." Both men guffawed. Neither noticed the tall horseman who was sitting on the slope opposite, watching.

Another rider appeared just as the stationmaster was about to reenter his shack. The train hooted, the trainman slammed his door shut, and the iron horse began to pick up speed. Whitey glanced up at the anxious arrival and nodded perfunctorily. He knew Lahood's foreman by sight.

"Morning, McGill. Just in time for the mail. Take me a minute to sort out the letters for the mine." He opened the sack preparatory to hunting through the bundle for the usual dozen or so missives that were destined for Lahood's camp.

Steadying his horse, the foreman leaned over to hand the stationmaster a slip of folded paper. "Hell with the mail. I'll come back for it later. The Boss wants you to send this telegram right away."

The stationmaster accepted the message, flipped it open, amd read silently. Then he shrugged and pocketed the paper.

"Really ought to get to the mail before—"

McGill leaned over a little farther, until his face was very close to the stationmaster's. "The Boss said, *right away*."

Whitey nodded, added a placating wave of his free hand. It wouldn't require much time to rid himself of the obligation. Men liked Lahood were always in such a damn hurry. Well, that wasn't his problem. He'd send the message, then settle in for a pleasant afternoon's perusal of everybody else's mail—or at least those envelopes he could open without being obvious about it. The stationmaster incurred no moral qualms over this blatantly illegal diversion. What else was there for a man in a solitary position to do on a slow afternoon in Lahood, California?

The foreman turned his horse around and headed back toward the hills. There was a last blast from the whistle of the southbound train as it rounded the far bend.

On the slope where a moment earlier there had been a single horseman there was now only brush and grass.

In another office elsewhere in the state another telegraph key began to chatter. The hand of the wizened old operator who managed this particular station functioned independently of his eyes and perhaps even of his mind. He'd worked as a telegrapher for so many years that he could understand the dots and dashes as clearly as any spoken language. The hand held a pencil and moved rapidly over a blank pad. For the benefit of customers not as conversant with Mr. Morse's symbology as he, it was required that he transcribe as well as translate.

Eventually the key stopped stuttering. The telegrapher double-checked his transcription, straightening the crooked h's and adding a flourish of punctuation. Then he slipped the paper into his pocket and hurried toward the door of his office.

A painted shingle surmounted the entrance.

TELEGRAPH

YUBA CITY POP. 2,301

The telegrapher scanned the street until he spotted a gap between the rush of wagons and horses, then deftly picked his way through to the other side. The building he was heading for also boasted a sign over the entrance.

U.S. MARSHAL

There were seven horses tied to the hitching rail that fronted the lawman's office. Each had a black saddle on its back. A black leather rifle holster slashed at an angle on the right-hand side of each seat. Their oiled walnut stocks gleaming, seven Winchesters filled the holsters. Expensive guns, worth a lot of money in a bustling frontier community like Yuba City. They sat there in plain sight, apparently unguarded. There was nothing to prevent a resourceful thief from making off with the lot of them.

Nothing except knowing better.

The old man hesitated outside the door to the office, nervously cleared his throat. He crossed himself reflexively, then knocked. He disliked leaving the familiar surroundings of his office, and he especially disliked leaving it to come here, but delivering was as much a part of his job as transcribing. Still, it was the one aspect of his employment he would have preferred to delegate to someone else. He knocked again.

This time the door was opened.

Hull Barret knocked a second time on the door of the shanty.

"Preacher? You awake?" Still no response. He pushed open the door and peered inside. It was true that he hadn't known their visitor for more than a couple of days, but he didn't strike Hull as the sort of man who made it a habit to sleep in.

His eyes scanned the familiar environs. The shanty was spotless and empty.

Worried as well as confused, he shut the door carefully and jogged around to the back. The lean-to he'd built there to serve as a stable was also deserted. His own horse grazed peacefully nearby, tethered to a stake by a long rope. He eyed the empty stable for a long moment, then turned and started toward the cabin closest to his.

Megan made a few final adjustments to the four place settings on the table, then seated herself. Her mother pivoted away from the stove and began ladling out eggs and beans. She handled the bulky cast-iron skillet easily with one hand.

"Are you all right this morning, Megan?"

The subject of her inquiry continued to stare at her plate. "I'm all right, Mother. Are you all right?"

The sharpness of her daughter's tone took Sarah slightly aback, but she didn't have time to question her further because footsteps sounded on the porch outside. Hull entered and quickly scanned the cabin's interior. Sarah noticed the anxious look on his face and instantly forgot about her daughter's puzzling behavior.

"Hello, Hull. Is something wrong?"

"He's gone."

"What? Who's gone?" She put the skillet back on the stove.

"The Preacher. I've been all through the camp looking for him. Nobody's seen him since last night. His stuff's missing from my place.'' He looked as though he was unable to believe his own words. "He's packed and left."

Sarah could only stare at him in disbelief, stunned by this unexpected development. "But why? Where to?"

Hull closed the door behind him. "I don't know," he told her dully. "He didn't say anything to me about it. Not a word. Nor to anyone else, near as I can find out. Nobody saw him ride out, either. He must've left before sun-up."

Megan Wheeler had nothing to add to the conversation. She sat motionless and stared guiltily at her steaming breakfast. Suddenly her mother's eggs and beans didn't seem as appetizing as usual. Occasionally she would sneak a glance at the adults, but she needn't have worried about her expression giving her away. Hull and her mother were much too concerned with the tragedy-in-the-making to pay any attention to her.

Nor was she the only one in the room experiencing feelings of guilt. Similar emotions were stirring inside her mother.

"Well, he—he probably went to tell Lahood how the vote went last night."

"With his bedroll and coat?"

Sarah had no immediate response to that, and finally she muttered, "I can't believe he just—left. I mean, it's not—not like him. We were his friends. He said so. After all he's gone and done for us, for him to just pick up and disappear—I can't believe that. If he was leaving he'd have told us something. He'd have . . ." Her voice trailed off helplessly.

Because no matter how she wished to believe otherwise, it remained that they *didn't* know what the Preacher was really like, any more than they had the slightest notion of what motivated him. He'd ridden in on them unannounced, had said as little as possible about himself, and now he'd decided to ride on. What was so strange about that? In its own unpleasant way it made perfect sense.

But she still refused to believe it.

Hull took a seat at the table and stared at his food. The world that had seemed so promising last night was beginning to contract around him, to strangle him.

"I expect we'll survive," he mumbled. "Somehow." There was little conviction in his tone.

"All that talk of fighting," Sarah's voice was brittle. "No wonder he left."

"What?" Hull frowned darkly. "What's that supposed to mean?"

She sat down opposite him. "Lahood and Marshal Stockburn be damned. Isn't that what you decided last night? He knew this Stockburn. He knew of his reputation, at least. And you all decide to fight instead of accepting Lahood's offer, and that next morning he's disappeared. Isn't it obvious?"

"That doesn't make any sense. I told you how he handled McGill and the other two."

"McGill isn't a Marshal, and two of Lahood's animals aren't deputies."

Hull refused to concede her point. "I can't believe that's why he left."

"Why not? I can't believe he left at all. And it would've been so simple if you hadn't convinced everyone to stay and fight."

Hull forced himself to maintain a civil tone. "I spoke my mind, if that's what you mean."

"You got the rest of them to vote your way, didn't you? They wanted to take the money, to accept Lahood's offer, pull up stakes, and start over again someplace else where people can live without being shot at. But you had to go and talk them out of it, Hull Barret."

"They voted their conscience. If you think I was the only one who wanted to stay and fight from the start, you're wrong."

"Oh sure," she said sarcastically. "There was you, and there was that crazy old fool Spider Conway. What does it matter to him if he gets killed? He's lived his life and he knows he isn't going to strike it rich, so why not go out in a blaze of glorious gunfire like a character from a ten-penny novel? Him and his war stories!"

"Every man voted the way he felt, Sarah."

"They voted to fight after you talked them into it! Against a bunch of professional killers!"

"If that's what it should come down to, you're damn right they did!" Hull replied hotly. He was getting tired of being polite for no good reason.

Sarah's voice rose to match his in intensity. "You think they'd have voted that way before the Preacher came? You think they'd have voted that way if they'd known he wasn't going to be here for the fight?"

"They voted to stick together! Like we always have."

She laughed bitterly. "Sure! Like Ulrik Lindquist and the rest who had the sense to leave 'stuck together.' The Preacher was holding them together, and that's all. They knew how he helped you in town. They watched him whip that—that animal that Lahood brought out here. They were counting on him to whip Lahood himself! All of you have been counting on that."

"I reckon I did all right by us before he came, didn't I?" Hull said stiffly as he rose from his chair. Sarah rose to confront him. She didn't get the chance.

The explosion rattled the windows and shook the cabin to its fragile foundation. Echoes of it rumbled down the canyon, bouncing off the reflective walls of granite before they faded away into the distance. But not before both Hull and Sarah grasped its significance.

The miner bolted from his place and threw the door aside in his hurry to get out onto the porch. Sarah and Megan crowded out behind him. The explosion had come from the upper end of the canyon. All eyes were turned in that direction. They were not alone. From the other shanties and shelters and cabins the other inhabitants of Carbon Canyon emerged to stare fearfully in the direction of the massive blast.

A huge cloud of dust rose from somewhere far upstream. Dogs and children were running in panic: the children to their homes, the dogs for the nearest hidey-hole. Megan saw them and thought of Linsey. The dust fanned out and began to settle.

The one person who probably knew better than anyone else in the canyon what the explosion portended was Spider Conway. His was the first gaze to drop from the distant reaches of the canyon to the creekbed where he'd been working. Sure enough, the strong current was already ebbing. The water level fell as he stared. In less time than a greenhorn would've thought possible, the rush of cold water had fallen to a listless trickle.

No water in the creek meant no way to placer mine; no panning, no sluicing, no washing of gravel. A man couldn't work a placer claim by walking along and picking out the minuscule flecks with his eyes. In its own way the presence of water was as vital as the presence of gold.

Spider directed a glob of tobacco juice into the inch-deep water. "Damned if that don't cut it," he muttered resignedly.

Hull Barret came to the same conclusion a moment later.

"That's it." There was a great tiredness in his voice. "It's all over, it's finished. Lahood's gone and damned up the creek, maybe even diverted it down that little side canyon east of here a half a mile upstream. Ain't a damn thing we can do about it either, because we've got no claim to the land above the Gossage diggings."

"Why can't you and Ev and everyone else just go up there and dig through the dirt?" Megan wanted to know.

He tried to smile at her, but failed dismally. "We could—if we didn't have to work under Lahood's guns. Remember, he has as much right to be up there as we do. We wouldn't have the protection of the law on our side if it came to a gunfight over headwater rights to the creek. Lahood didn't go to the trouble of diverting it so we could walk up there and get our water back.

"Oh sure, the Mining Commission down in Sacramento might side with us, but it'd take 'em weeks, months to make up their minds and come to a decision on it—if Lahood didn't buy 'em off first. He doesn't really have to worry about that, though, and he knows it. Because ain't none of us can last that long without a few sacks of dust to buy beans and flour. Leastwise, none of the families can. Once they give up and leave, Lahood'll be able to push out or buy out any that stay behind. Oh, he's got it all figured out, the sonofabitch!"

Sarah's eyes were glistening with tears. She stared up at him accusingly. "If you'd accepted his offer this wouldn't have happened. We'd all be clear of it now and with some real money in our pockets. How much do you think Lahood's going to offer for our claims now!" Unable to control her sobs any longer, she whirled and ran back inside. Megan followed, her eyes unable to meet Hull's, her expression blank.

Abandoned, Hull turned his attention back to the creek. There was hardly enough water running down it now to mirror the fear, doubt, and confusion in his face.

It was a bank of substance. You could tell that by the oiled walnut paneling that surrounded the tellers' cages, from the polished brass rails that offered surcease to tired feet, and by the imported cut and beveled glass cases that displayed works of art for the enjoyment and edification of waiting patrons. It was a bank that had been founded on gold and was now supported by farming and ranching, more mundane but equally profitable enterprises. It was not a bank for everyone.

The teller's appearance was a reflection of his status. His suit was freshly laundered and pressed, his white shirt spotless, both loops of the bowtie that secured his collar of equal length. At the moment he was methodically counting out greenbacks for the elegantly dressed matron standing before him. It was no small measure of the confidence its customers had in this bank that they agreed to accept their money in paper instead of coin.

"Twenty-three, twenty-four, twenty-five. Thank you, Mrs. Green, and I do hope your mother is feeling better. Please give her my regards."

"I shall certainly do that, Mr. Wrather."

He checked his drawer, said automatically, "Next, please," and tried to conceal his surprise when he finally looked up at the figure standing patiently before him. He noted the thin line of a mouth, the oddly unsettling eyes, and the reassuring white collar.

"Afternoon, Reverend. What can I do for you?"

Wordlessly, the tall man slid his hand under the grille.

When it withdrew there was a key on the smooth hardwood in front of the clerk. The younger man nodded briskly.

"If you'll follow me, Reverend. It's around—"

"I know the way," the customer said quietly.

The clerk smiled. "Yes, of course." He led the keyholder around the line of teller windows, past the vice-president's desk, to meet him at the swinging doors. A single nod in the direction of the guard granted them entrance to the gaping vault.

The teller ran his finger down the fourth in a seemingly endless parade of safe deposit boxes until he located the one that matched up with the key he'd been given. "Here we are."

He inserted the key into the left-hand keyhole, then placed his own master key into the matching receptacle on the right and twisted both keys simultaneously. The door clicked open. He pocketed the master and returned the other key to its owner.

The black metal box slid out easily and he immediately turned it over to the customer. "Here you are, Reverend."

Accepting the box, the Preacher turned to enter a small curtained booth. The teller watched him for a moment. It was his experience that the vast run of reverends was more voluble than the average customer, whereas this specimen of that particular breed bordered on the mute. Not that it was any of his business. He shrugged and began hunting through his pockets for a toothpick while keeping an eye on the entrance to the vault in the event that Mr. Higgins or one of his other superiors should chance to enter. He was enjoying the respite from his telling duties at the window (a little bank humor there) and in any event he doubted that whatever the minister had to do in his private cubicle would take very long.

In this he was quite correct, but if he'd been permitted to observe the nature of what was transpiring behind the black privacy curtain, it's doubtful he would ever have forgotten it.

The Preacher set the safe deposit box down on the bench in front of him. Fingers deftly unfastened the single latch that secured the lid.

Inside was a chamois-wrapped bundle. Carefully the Preacher set to unwrapping it. Beneath the protective cloth was a well-worn .44 with a staghorn grip. He picked the weapon up. The handle was cold against his palm. The vault was not heated at night and it was still early. He studied the oiled steel and prised lightly at the trigger.

Then he put it down on the bench while he fumbled with his shirt. The chamois went back into the box. There was nothing to wrap in it. The white collar he added to the otherwise empty container fit neatly into a corner.

Not everyone felt the need to personally inspect the trickle that had recently been the fast-flowing mountain stream called Carbon. Hull Barret was one of them, though. Standing next to him as they walked through the exposed creek bed was Spider Conway. Behind them came a pair of ancient sourdoughs named Bossy and Biggs. Having already committed himself to the defense of his claim (perhaps a bit more vociferously than now seemed prudent), Ev Gossage joined them as well. So did Jake Henderson.

They had vowed to stand and fight Coy Lahood, but their adversary had slyly confronted them with a virtual *fait accompli*. No water meant no placer mining. Lahood had beaten them without having to fire a shot.

"Shit," Bossy muttered as he gazed despairingly at the dried-up creekbed. Having given up the thought of striking it big six years ago when he'd first come to the Sierras, he would have been more than satisfied to eke out an existence in Carbon Canyon. Now it appeared even that was to be denied him. Rotten bad luck he'd always had, and still he'd managed to retain his optimism toward life and enthusiasm for mining. But this latest catastrophe threatened to push him over into the dour ranks of the doomsayers.

Henderson was no less discouraged. "Well, I reckon it's time to pack up the missus and light out."

Gossage readily agreed with him. "It sure don't seem we got much choice. Near as I can figure it, we're licked. I warn't sure Lahood was too tough for us, but I'm about convinced he's too smart for us." He looked to the man standing silently in front of him. Spider Conway nodded once, then spoke to the same quiet figure.

"What about you, Barret? Any ideas?"

A dull expression on his face, Hull shook his head while continuing to gaze in silence at the stream. Conway looked past him, upslope in the direction of his fellow miner's cabin.

"Where's the Preacher? He'll know what to do. Bet it don't come out of the good book, neither." He forced a chuckle as he looked back at Hull. "If he's still restin' up at your place, let's go and see what he's got to say about this. He's probably been lyin' up there thinkin' on it and waitin' for us to come and ask him." The old miner started uphill. The movement, more than anything he'd said, snapped Hull out of his silent reverie.

"Save your legs, Spider. He ain't up there."

Conway halted, his boots sinking into exposed river sand. "Well then, where? He go into town? I didn't see him go into town." He surveyed the others. "Any of you boys see the Preacher leave this morning?" There were negative headshakes all around.

"He didn't go into town," Hull informed them. "Leastwise, I don't think he did."

"Well then, where is he?" Conway demanded to know.

Hull shot him a discouraged look. "He ain't here."

Ev Gossage finally unraveled what Hull was trying, but unable, to say. "You mean he's gone?"

"Well, I ain't sure—I mean, not exactly." Conscious that all eyes were on him again, Hull thought fast. "I expect he, uh, went in to tell Lahood that we turned him down."

Gossage and Henderson exchanged a glance while Biggs looked confused, as though he'd heard what Hull had said but couldn't quite square it with what he knew to be reasonable. But none of them called Hull's bluff. There was no reason to challenge the other man's assumption. After all, wasn't he the Preacher's closest friend, and wouldn't he be the one most likely to know what the Preacher was likely to do?

"Well, that makes sense—I guess," Henderson murmured.

"Sure," agreed Bossy. "Somebody had to tell Lahood. I'm just glad nobody nominated me."

"Nobody'd nominate you to catch dogs," his partner growled.

His confidence boosted by the lack of a challenge, Hull decided to play out his string a little further. "But before he left, he said that if anything happened while he was away, we should try and do like he'd do if he was still here."

"Shit." Bossy's vocabulary being somewhat limited, the old sourdough relied more on shifts in inflection to convey his feelings instead of a change of expletives.

Ev Gossage looked suddenly thoughtful, as if marginally

inspired by Hull's ambiguous reassurance that the Preacher would return soon. "I don't know. Suppose we *could* dry-pan for a couple of days, come to think of it."

"Why not?" Henderson indicated the feeble remnant of the creek. "Somebody might get lucky and find some color in the rocks. You can't pan in water that's over your belt. This is our chance to find out what's been swept into the middle of the creekbed."

"That's it!" Hull said with mock enthusiasm. "I know he'd hate to see us quit without we gave it our best."

"I dunno." Biggs was older than the rest of them, and therefore not nearly as hopeful. "Dry-panning's awful hard work. I never knew a man made the price o' a sack of flour doin' it."

"Aw, come on, Biggs," Henderson urged him, "let's play her out for a couple of days. What can we lose? And the Preacher'll figure something out when he gets back."

"Sure...that's right...the Preacher'll know what to do..." the men murmured encouragingly to each other.

"Won't he, Hull?" Gossage asked the older man with the benign naïveté of ever hopeful youth.

"Sure he will, Ev," Hull replied blandly.

"One nugget." Spider was already scanning the sand and rocks with new intensity. "Like to find me one big nugget. I'd shove it so far up Coy Lahood's ass it'd wink at him when he washed his teeth."

Gossage let out a whoop. "You tell 'em, Spider! Come on, Jake!" He led Henderson in a dash up the hill toward their cabins to break the news to the womenfolk that the situation was well if temporarily in hand. Their lives would go on as usual—at least for a few more days. Stability and a sense of immediate purpose lent the younger men courage.

Spider Conway, however, was not so easily fooled. He was neither as gullable as Henderson and Gossage nor as feeble-minded as the easy-going Bossy and Biggs. He hung back until he was alone with Barret in the creek. Then he turned those sharp eyes on his companion.

"You got sand, Barret, and I admire you for that. I admire you for aimin' to stick it out, too, but it's a damn good thing you're just a miner and ain't runnin' for mayor of this non-town, because you can't lie worth a damn."

Hull essayed a sickly smile and pretended to examine a chunk of quartz. "I don't know what you're gettin' at, Spider."

"Is that a fact? Listen to me, Barret. You're a good man, but you ain't the kind to play the fool or the martyr. That's better left to worn-out old horse's behinds like me, and to my boys, who don't know no better. I can see the lay o' the land and I expect so can you.

"With the Preacher gone and Lahood on the warpath, your life won't be worth spit around here. Don't throw it away on this bunch." He nodded contemptuously toward the ram-shackle collection of cabins and shanties. "You don't owe them a thing, and you got as much or more than most of 'em to live for. If I was you, I'd pack up them two ladies and *git*."

"I ain't the runnin' kind, Spider."

"Hell, this wouldn't be like runnin'. Grant wasn't runnin' when he pulled back to regroup in the West. This'd be common sense. It's what I'd do now if I were in your boots."

Hull hesitated. "What are you going to do, Spider, if—if he doesn't come back?"

The old miner spat into the sand. "Me, I been here too long to run." He grinned around his chaw. "My mouth works better than my legs, anyways. I'll stick it out whatever comes. But just because I'm a pig-headed old fart don't mean you have to try and be one too."

Having said his piece, Conway turned on his heel and strode off downstream, picking his way through the exposed rocks toward his claim. Hull looked after him for a bit, pondering his words. Then he let out a tired sigh and started climbing the rubble-strewn slope toward Sarah Wheeler's cabin.

Megan saw him coming. She was standing next to the first trees. There was no point in her descending to greet him. It was her mother he'd want to be talking to anyways, and now there was little comfort to be gained from his presence, though he was a nice enough man and had always been good to her.

Nor would it do any good to go inside to talk to her mother before Hull arrived. There was no longer much comfort to be gained from that quarter, either. She suspected it was part of growing up, and it was one aspect of maturing she didn't much like. There was a time when a single word or two from her mother could wipe away all life's misfortunes and make everything seem fresh and good again.

No longer. She'd changed, was changing as she stood there and stared at the eerily silent creek. And now the Preacher was gone, too.

Something close to her feet caught her attention. She bent to pluck the dandelion, held it close to her face. Once it would have delighted her with its delicate beauty. She was too sad now to be delighted by anything. A puff and the gossamer plumes exploded into the air, needing only the wind to free them.

It just wasn't fair. Nothing seemed fair anymore. She let the stem fall to the earth and ground it underfoot.

IX

Everyone was hard at work on their claims the following morning, only now they no longer had the power of Carbon Creek to assist them. Dry mining was every bit as difficult as Biggs had claimed.

Ev Gossage dumped shovelfuls of gravel into his sluice. His wife Bess followed each with a bucket of water gleaned from the forlorn watercourse's meager remaining supply. Ev knew she couldn't keep up that heavy work for more than an hour or two. There were still the household chores to attend to. But the hour passed, and the second, and both husband and wife kept at it, not knowing what else to do but work until they couldn't work anymore.

Biggs and Bossy had staked out the largest remaining pool to pan, but without a steady current to keep the water clear one of them had to stir the muck constantly while the other searched for color. Jake Henderson had sat down nearby. He dejectedly held his head in his hands, having given up already with his soul if not his body.

Having no wife to fetch water for him, Hull Barret had to load his Long Tom with gravel, then put his shovel aside to pick up his bucket. Each trip to the remaining water and back put an additional, unaccustomed strain on the muscles of his back and arms, but there was no other way to work the sluice, and that was still more efficient than panning.

He dumped the bucketful into the wooden trough, washing the gravel over the riffles. Three or four buckets of water to each shovelful of gravel. It hardly seemed worth the effort. He had to keep working, though, if for no other reason than to set an example for the others. In the absence of the Preacher they'd come to look up to him. If he quit now, there wouldn't be a family left in Carbon Canyon by nightfall. Only Spider Conway, who was too stubborn to quit, and his boys, who were too stupid to know better.

A slim figure appeared to stare at him while he worked. Laboring over the Long Tom with single-minded concentration, he failed to notice her until she spoke to him.

"Hull?"

He spared Megan the briefest of glances, acknowledging her presence with a grunt without interrupting the rhythm of his work.

"Hull, are you angry with me?"

"Nuh-uh," he said abstractedly, gritting his teeth as he tossed another heavy shovelful of gravel and sand into the upper end of the sluice box. "What gave you that notion?"

She shrugged. "I dunno. You angry at Mama, then?"

Frowning, he straightened and leaned on his shovel for support. He knew enough about young'uns Megan's age to know that the sooner he let her say what she'd come to say, the sooner she'd leave him to get back to his work in peace. His shirt was sopping with sweat and his face and arms were begrimed with mud. The contrast with Megan, standing there in her spotless white skirt and blouse, was profound. He found time enough to note that the elaborate coiffure she'd affected the day before apparently had been more trouble than it had been worth. Once more her hair was secured by simple pigtails.

"No, I wouldn't say that. No, not exactly angry."

Megan nodded sagely, striving to look older than her fifteen years. "She hurt your feelings, didn't she? I know what that feels like. 'If you love something, set it free. If it returns to you, it's yours. If it doesn't, it never was.'"

Hull blinked at her, curious as to the origin of this little speech but too tired to press for elaboration. "I guess so." He hefted his shovel. "We'll talk later, huh? I've got a lot of work to do." He attacked the loose material of the creekbed with the point of the shovel.

For a few more minutes Megan watched quietly as he worked the Long Tom, loading it with gravel and then washing the contents with buckets of creek water. She said not another word, which suited Hull just fine. Here lately, talking to women seemed to get him into more trouble than it was worth.

"Can I borrow the mare?" she said abruptly.

Again Hull paused. If he'd been less exhausted, less preoccupied with other thoughts, he might have thought to ask why. Instead all he said was, "Can you saddle her by yourself?"

Megan looked abashed. "I already did."

"Sure, take her out for a stretch," he replied indifferently. "She gets bored grazing outside the stable all day and she'd probably be grateful for the run."

He was rewarded with a bright smile. "Thanks, Hull." She turned and scampered off up the hill.

If only I had that kind of energy, he mused. He dumped another shovelful of gravel into the sluice and then picked up the bucket. After spreading the gravel as best he could with his hand he stumbled back to the creek for still another bucketload.

Unencumbered, his mind went back to the days when he'd first heard the wondrous tales of gold in California, the stories of men picking up nuggets big as hen's eggs off the ground and of others raking up gold flakes like fallen leaves. Now he wondered how he could ever have been so gullible. He didn't feel especially bad, though, because the Sierra foothills were full of thousands like him who'd heard and believed those same stories.

He'd prepared as well as possible, reading the right books (which, it developed, were invariably written by men who'd never lifted anything heavier than a pen and had never been farther west than St. Louis), listening to the stories, taking notes on the rights and the wrongs of mining.

Ah, the stories! He'd listened raptly to tales of savage Indians only to discover that hardly any Indians remained. They had been effectively wiped out by the white man's diseases instead of his weapons, and the sorry remnants he glimpsed begging in towns and by the wayside hardly seemed the kith and kin of the great Sioux and Cheyenne.

He'd heard stories of miners having to eat their horses and mules and finally each other in order to survive the long Sierra winter. He'd memorized hearsay on how to deal with claim jumpers and crooked gamblers, with mosquitoes the size of field mice and bears that had to be shot twelve times just to slow them down. And unlike many, he'd even prepared himself to deal with lies, just in case everything he was overhearing turned out to be somewhat less than God's truth.

But the one thing no one had thought to warn him about or instruct him how to cope with was the everlasting, unending boredom of the actual work of mining itself.

He dipped the bucket into a pool of stagnant water just as an ear-splitting cry resounded through the canyon.

Having no gun, he made a run for his shovel, only to slow when he located the source of the shout. Spider Conway was pirouetting about his claim, waving his ancient floppy chapeau over his head and dancing a wild, frenetic sarabande like a man being assailed by hornets. Nor was he screaming a warning, as Hull initially feared. His dance, like his words, was purely celebratory.

"Rich, by Christ! Sweet Mary Holy Ghost Mother of God I've struck 'er rich!"

Whooping and hollering and whirling about like a man possessed, as indeed he was, Conway was holding something the size and shape of a loaf of bread. He kept tossing it from one hand to the other as his exultant voice reverberated off the sides of Carbon Canyon.

"Gossage! Henderson, Barret, look at this!" He held the lump over his head for all to see. "Eddy and Teddy, you pair of clodpoles, come and see what your daddy's pulled outta the stream!" He turned abruptly so that he was facing down the creek and shook his prize in the direction of the distant foothills.

"Lahood, you son-of-a-bitch, you mush-mouthed offspring of a rancid sow, I beat you! Look at this. Old Spider's struck it rich!"

Across the stream Bossy and Biggs ceased their panning to view this extraordinary spectacle. Though older and more experienced than Spider, they had none of his savvy. Why, Conway could read, and even write his own name, and in most matters the two elderly partners usually deferred to their compatriot's greater knowledge.

But now they hesitated, wondering if their mate had, like

148

the train that came from Sàcramento three times a week, gone 'round the bend.

"What's that lump you holdin', Conway?" Biggs called out uncertainly. "Some kind o' turtle?"

"Turtle my ass!" Conway laughed and continued his dance, brandishing the precious lump like a weapon. "It's a lump of aggregate, ya crazy old fart! Mother lode aggregate. Never seen anything like it. Quartz and gold, and damned if there ain't some silver and lead in it, too. Chock full o' nuggets. Can't even count 'em, they's too many!" He finally ran down like an old clock spring and stood there in the shallow water, staring in wonder at his discovery. He was holding it so tightly his fingers were starting to turn white.

"Shit," Bossy murmured in amazement. The two old miners exchanged a look, then threw their tools aside in their haste to scurry through the rocks toward Conway's claim.

Eddy and Teddy beat them to their father's side. Both boys stared down at the chunk of matrix. "What you got there, Dad?" Teddy mumbled, gazing at the lump with wide-eyed innocence.

"What's it look like, y'brainless barn owl? It's gold! More gold than you're likely to see the rest of your life, unless there's more like it right under our feet." Conway tossed his prize into the air and caught it, marveling at its weight.

"Glory be, but if I don't think it's half gold." He looked up at both his benumbed offspring. "Well don't just stand there lookin' like a pair of damn statues. Run and git the mules. We're goin' to town."

"Us?" Teddy gaped at him in disbelief.

"Going to town?" Eddy added.

"You're damn right 'us.' The Conways are goin' to have them a little celebration." There was a gleam in his eye that didn't come from the gold. "Wouldn't be right for us to keep this little find to ourselves. It's only fair that we share it with our neighbors. Now git along with you two and hitch up the wagon."

Hull was watching from his own claim across the creekbed. He was enjoying the celebration almost as much as if the discovery had been his. He'd known Conway ever since he'd first decided to try his luck on Carbon Creek. The old man had provided the newcomer with invaluable practical advice, giving freely of the lore he'd accumulated over the years and asking nothing in return. If anyone deserved to make a big strike, it was Spider.

So Hull Barret was happy for his friend's success, happy in the knowledge that at least one of them would get out with something more than blisters and memories to show for the many months of back-breaking toil and dull, repetitive work. As for himself, well, it was said that such luck rarely smiled upon more than one miner in ten square miles of claims, and that was back in the boom days of '49 and '50.

Movement upslope drew his attention. Sarah had come out of her cabin, carrying a big basket of laundry. She hesitated briefly to gaze down at the celebratory scene that was taking place at Spider's claim. Then she turned away and crossed to her clothesline.

Of course, he reflected, it was also said that a man makes his own luck. Weren't there other things worth working for besides gold? So often the yellow metal proved a false mistress to its discoverers. What was it Megan had told him? Something about love, and letting go, and coming back? He shook his head, then wiped sweat from his brow with the back of an arm as he watched Sarah set out her washing.

Several of the seemingly unrelated thoughts that were

swimming around loose inside his brain suddenly snapped together as neatly as a clipper ship's rigging. He let the bucket he was holding drop, oblivious to the water that spilled from it, and started climbing the hill. Spider's whoops and yells echoed in his ears.

She was pinning the laundry to the line the same as she always did, working slowly and methodically, placing each piece of washing precisely an inch from its neighbor to maximize the room on the line. So intent was she on her work and her own inner thoughts that she failed to notice his approach. He stood there quietly watching her work. Initial certainty gave way in her presence to confusion, which was eventually replaced by determination.

"Sarah?"

One hand froze in the process of securing a pair of bloomers to the line with a well-worn wooden pin. She did not look back, but resumed her work. Seeing that she wasn't going to say anything, Hull decided to dive in all the way. If he retreated now without saying what he'd come to say, he'd not only damage his chances further, he'd leave looking like a fool. More than anything else in his life, he didn't want to look like a fool in front of Sarah Wheeler. He intended to have his say.

"I wanted to apologize if anything I've done or said is going to stand between us. I've taken a lot these past weeks. I don't think I could handle thinking that, on top of everything else that's happened."

"Can't think of any such." Her reply was delivered in an even, uninflected voice devoid of emotion.

The silence and the significance of the moment were too much for Hull, an essentially uncomplicated man. Mining was a direct business. He was not used to dealing with subtleties. Unsure how to proceed, he glanced down toward the creek and nodded.

"Look's like Spider's payday's come."

She turned to follow his stare, sounding noncommittal. "Maybe it was just his turn. Like it was your turn a couple of days ago. Everybody takes their turn, I guess."

"Yeah, well, leastwise somebody's gonna say goodbye to Carbon Canyon a few dollars richer."

"Looks like."

This time the silence was longer. Not knowing what else to do, Hull moved closer to her. She stepped clear and began to hang Megan's dress, not so much ignoring him as she was professing disinterest. There was no indication of malice in her movements, but neither was there anything resembling encouragement.

"When we all pack up to leave," Hull told her, "I hope you know there's plenty of space in my wagon for," he gestured toward her cabin, "for whatever you're wantin' to take."

She spoke without looking back at him. "Are you asking us to leave here with you?"

"I reckon we're all leavin', ain't we?" he replied evasively.

To this she said nothing. Then there were no more clothes to hang. As she turned to leave, he ducked under the clothesline and confronted her face to face.

"Dammit, Sarah, ever since your Daddy died I've done what I could. I helped you and Megan as best I knew how and never put any conditions on it. Well now I'm puttin' one. You owe me the truth. What have you got against me?"

"Nothing." Her reply was barely audible.

"What's that?" He moved as close to her as the clothesline would allow.

"Nothing. I don't have nothing against you."

He didn't dare smile. He was still unable to believe, still unsure whether to press the issue to its inevitable conclusion.

Oh hell, he told himself, why not? Get it over with one way or the other. He'd lost everything else during a year of being unsure. Lahood had put finish to the community of Carbon Creek. It was time the last loose ends were tied up.

"Well then," he asked, rather more brusquely than he intended, "do you love me or not?"

She raised her face to meet his eyes and this time, unlike on so many similar occasions in the recent past, he didn't flinch from that unblinking examination. She took note of that, just as she took note of the pain and hope he displayed so guilelessly on his handsome face. And after a long moment, she nodded.

"You're the decentest man I've ever known, Hull Barret. You've watched over me and mine and took care of us when any other man would've tried to take advantage. It took me a long time to believe you were sincere in what you were doin' for us. I blame myself for that. I've had a hard time believing in any man since—since Megan's father ran out on us." She put a hand on his cheek. It was smooth and warm. She smiled up at him.

"I expect it's been rough on you. Since that man weren't around no more I've tended to take out all my bitterness on you, and you don't deserve that. You deserve a lot better. Yes, Hull, I do love you. I have for some time now, but the old hurt made me keep it locked up tight inside. The hurt, and the bitterness. You're gentle and kind and caring, Hull. I saw that right from the start. I just never could let it out and—I wanted to be sure. For Megan's sake even more than mine."

She pressed up tightly against him and he put his arms around her to hold her close. "I wish I were better with words, Sarah, but I never was. I always kind o' dance around what I'm tryin' to say without knowin' how to come out and say it. With a woman, anyways, and especially with you."

Her eyes shut tightly as she clung to him, the tension that had existed between them shattered for all time. "I'm so sorry, Hull, so sorry. I apologize for being so high-strung lately. It's just that I've—I've been so confused." As she spoke she was looking past him, at the room where until this morning the Preacher had stayed.

It was just as well for both of them that Hull construed her remark as a reflection of his own recent frame of mind. He nodded sympathetically.

"What with everything that's been goin' on around here it's a wonder we ain't all crazy. But it'll be all right now, Sarah. You'll see. I'm goin' to make it all right for the three of us. There's nothin' more to worry about." He disengaged himself gently and gazed down into her upturned face.

"I ain't afraid of hard work. I guess not every man's destined to strike it rich, but that don't mean he can't make a decent livin' for himself and his family. We'll start over again someplace else. Maybe in Sacramento, or maybe we'll try San Francisco. And I hear tell there's even people startin'' to move south, to a little pueblo called Los Angeles. It'll be just fine so long as we're all together. There's always a place in the city for a man that's willin' to work hard.

"But there's somethin' else we got to do first. First town we get to we'll find ourselves another preacher. That's one bit of business I've got enough put aside to pay for." He chuckled softly and gazed beyond her, envisioning the ceremony as the fantasy he'd always dreamed of but never dared hope could be made reality.

He didn't see Sarah's eyes drop at the mention of the word *preacher*, nor the blush of shame that stained her cheeks. It faded quickly, however, almost as though she willed it away.

"Yes. Another preacher." She pulled him to her once again, locking her arms around him and squeezeing with all her might as if to force out every last trace of the conflicting emotions that had been tormenting her for the last few days.

Of all the tasks at the mine in which he participated, Josh Lahood's favorite was to scan the bottom of the forty-foot-long iron sluice for traces of color. The promise of gold enabled a man to shut out the roar of the monitor and the noise of drenched workers shoveling gravel and rock. Not only that, but when he was on collection duty he was usually able to pocket a small nugget or two without being seen. Even if he was, no one would dare report the theft to his father. The operation didn't depend for its survival on such minor discoveries. Besides, his father was tight with his money, and the gold Josh pocketed was a useful and necessary supplement to his regular allowance. What the old man didn't know wouldn't hurt him.

Today the sluice displayed flecks of dust and the occasional larger fragment, but no nuggets. He hadn't found one in more than a week, and now even dust was becoming scarce. Everyone knew what that portended. Cobalt Canyon was nearly played out, having yielded to the monitor and the sluice all the gold it possessed. The whole operation was going to have to be moved to more profitable diggings soon, or the company would find itself operating at a loss. Every man in Lahood's employ knew where their next destination was going to be. Just as soon as some minor difficulties were cleared up.

McGill arrived, dismounted near the far end of the sluice, and hurried to interrupt his boss. A couple of the shovel men glanced curiously in the direction of the conversation, though the steady roar of the monitor made it impossible to hear any of what was being said. It appeared to be good news, however, since both the foreman and Lahood's boy were grinning from ear to ear by the time McGill turned to point toward the trees that lined the far hillside.

Still grinning, the foreman assumed Josh's place at the sluice and watched while the boss's son loped toward the rail where his horse was tied. The rest of the men followed his progress until he was swallowed up by the forest. They chatted curiously among themselves as they worked. There was nothing up there but rocks and trees. Yet it was clear McGill had sent the younger man off in that direction with some purpose in mind. They were more than a little puzzled. But since McGill remained by the business end of the sluice and did not offer any explanations, there was nothing for the rest of them to do but attend to their work while continuing to speculate.

Josh guided his mount through the pines. It was quieter up on the hillside. The woods served to mute the monitor's thunder. Another rider was waiting to greet him, just as McGill had said. Josh strove to hide his surprise.

She looked very pretty indeed, sitting there atop her mare. She was as unexpected a sight as the sun in winter, and just as welcome.

"Well, Megan Wheeler, welcome to Cobalt Canyon." He managed a half bow from his saddle, then pulled up alongside her. "Come to see how the rich folks do it, huh?"

She shrugged, apparently indifferent. "Maybe."

"Your mom know where you are?" He looked beyond her, but there was no sign of another presence in the woods.

"I don't tell her everything," the girl told him haughtily. "I go where I want when I please."

"Well now, that's admirable. Bet she wouldn't like it, though, if she knew you were here."

"I'm almost sixteen. Same age as she was when she got married. I can do what I want. You think I have to ask her permission every time I want to take a step outside our cabin?"

He put up both hands in front of him. "Oh no, not me!" He was grinning broadly. "I mean, it's plain to me you're more'n able to take care of yourself." He jerked a thumb in the direction of the canyon below. "Long as you're here, maybe you'd like for me to show you around? It's why you came by, ain't it?"

"Maybe," she said again.

He turned his mount around and started downhill. "Come on then." She chucked the mare's reins and let it pick its own way as it followed Josh.

The younger Lahood was nothing if not an enthusiastic guide. As they emerged from the trees he pointed toward the upper end of the canyon.

"Three quarters of a mile upstream we diverted half of Cobalt Creek. See?" He chuckled. "Dad's an old hand with dynamite. He can make a creek do just about anything he wants it to." She gave no indication that this snide reference to recent events in Carbon Canyon made any impression on her, even though it was tantamount to an indirect confession.

"It flows through a ditch that runs along the contours of the slope, there, and ends a hundred yards up yonder, to our right.''

Megan tried to follow with her eyes. "It can't just *end*. The water has to go somewhere."

"Sure it does. It runs into a length of three-foot pipe over there," he pointed, "that heads almost straight down. See, there's ten yards of three-foot pipe. It narrows into a two-foot pipe and then into a one-footer. All the time the water's goin' downslope it's picking up speed, see, and it picks up force as the pipe gets thinner. Volume plus compression equals energy."

She shook her head. "I'm not sure I understand."

"I'm not sure I do either, but that's what Dad says."

They were off the hillside now and down in the bottom of the canyon. He led her toward the sluice and the monitor platform. Megan kept pace with her guide, fascinated in spite of herself by the complexity and scale of the Lahood operation.

"At the bottom of the far slope, over there," he went on, "all that water is funneled from the one-foot pipe into a four-inch-diameter hose. The hose connects up to the monitor. My dad brought in five boiler-makers to put the pipe together, and we bought the hose from a fire company in San Francisco. You got to hand it to Dad." He was forced to shout now in order to make himself heard.

"Every company in California trying to get monitor hose from the outfit that makes 'em back east, and here Dad goes and beats every one of 'em to the punch by buying the extra hose from a fire company, right out from under their noses. Ain't nobody yet ever beat Coy Lahood at cards or gold-mining." He looked over at her. "That's how we do it, Megan. What do you think of all this?"

"It hurts my ears." She put her hands to the sides of her head to illustrate what she was trying to tell him. It was so loud in the bottom of the canyon, this close to the water cannon, that she didn't see how anyone could hear themselves think, let alone talk. As for the monitor itself, it was impressive, yes, but also frightening. She hadn't imagined that it would be frightening.

Josh was used to the noise, however, just as he was used to communicating over the steady thunder. "When all that water leaves the monitor, it's going at two hundred pounds per square inch. Blasts the gravel right out of the cliff. The other half of Cobalt Creek runs right over here—right down the creek bed and through the sluice. So the creek does all the heavy work for us except for loading the gravel into the sluice bed."

Megan's eyes swept over the hillside where the monitor had played, taking in the barren rock, the awful man-made erosion, noting the absence of even the scrawniest vegetation. She'd overheard others talking about what the monitor could do to a canyon, but she hadn't really been able to envision the scope of the destruction. It was like something out of a nightmare. She tried to imagine what it would be like to have a water cannon working in Carbon Canyon, and shuddered.

"It looks like hell," she finally told him.

The comment had no effect whatsoever on Josh Lahood, who replied proudly, "We can placer twenty tons of gravel a day with this rig. And even after the equipment's all paid for and the crew is paid off and you allow for delays and breakdowns and repairs, there's still plenty of gold left over. This is how you make *real* money, Megan. Not beans and flour money, like the tin-pans in Carbon."

He pulled up. They were little more than a stone's throw from the monitor platform. Club leaned into the iron as he guided the nozzle over the opposite slope. The sluice was nearby. Three men were working there under McGill's supervision. All four of them were splitting their attention between their work and the pair of riders. Their expressions were anticipatory and unpleasant. Megan did't notice them. Her thoughts were elsewhere.

She was snapped back to reality as Josh Lahood reached over to grab the reins away from her. He pulled her mount close to his own, then leaned toward her. His face was dominated by that engaging and yet somehow reptilian smile.

"Now you've had your little tour, you've seen what our operation's like. You can tell me what you really come by for."

There was something new in his voice that hadn't been there before. It caused Megan to look sharply at him. "I—I was just out riding, and I thought I'd see for myself what everybody else's been talking about."

"Well I can understand that. It's nice to look at what you ain't seen on your own before. I've been wanting a closer look at something too." His smile widened.

She shook her head, her expression full of sudden fear and the confusion of innocence. It only served to stimulate Lahood all the more. "I don't understand. You've seen me before."

"Yeah, but not up close. Real close."

Her eyes widened. She turned away from him and tried to spur the mare forward, but it was too late. It had been too late for several minutes now, she realized suddenly. This wasn't Carbon Canyon and Josh Lahood—Josh Lahood wasn't a well-meaning neighbor. Dark tales and indirect warnings whispered to her at night by her mother flooded in on her. She'd paid little attention to any of them, supremely confident in her own ability to handle any situation she might find herself in.

All that confidence had vanished like smoke. She tried to wrench the reins away from Lahood's fingers. As she leaned toward him he bent over to wrap both arms around her. She fought against him, batting futilely at his head and shoulders as he hauled her onto his knee. His strength was frightening, and there was sinister purpose behind every movement he made.

His hands were moving and she couldn't stop them from searching out all the secret places. She was too shocked and ashamed to cry out. Then he was kissing her, but it wasn't the way she'd imagined it should be. He was attacking her with his lips, wet and possessive. There was no suggestion of affection in any of his actions. It was an assault, sharp and unpleasant. She thought back to what she'd been told, to the stories she'd overheard, and she knew that worse than unsought kisses were to come.

There was nothing she could do, but she kept trying to fight anyway. Struck by her wildly kicking feet, the mare bolted. Even if anyone had been present to come to her aid, they couldn't have heard her screams over the rumble of the monitor.

Her gyrations and blows panicked Lahood's own mount. It pivoted and charged off upstream. Some of Lahood's pleasure was muted as his horse broke for rough ground. He couldn't control the gelding and his prize at the same time. They started to gallop past the platform, heading for the devastated upper reaches of the canyon.

"Clubbb!" he yelled.

The giant heard the cry. The instant he saw what was happening, he spun the water cannon around. The powerful stream of water cut off the gelding's headlong dash. A dozen miners dove wildly for safety as the bone-crushing flow

161

swerved in their direction. Others scrambled to surround Josh Lahood's wheeling, wild-eyed mount.

Soaked to the skin and laughing like a madman, Josh finally got his skittish steed under control. He slid from the saddle with Megan clasped tightly to him, stumbled, and recovered his footing on the muddy ground. The roughnecks and roustabouts who worked for his father began to crowd close. They had found something more worthy of their attention than the gyrations of the monitor.

"Lookit what I got me, boys. A tin-pan's daughter!"

"Let me go!" Megan was terrified and furious all at the same time.

"Ain't she purty," one of the men murmured, staring at her out of the muck that covered his face.

"Where'd you find 'er, boss?" another inquired.

"Why hell, Carlos, she just rode on in of her own free will. McGill told me she was curious t'see what we got here." That brought forth some unpleasant guffaws from the circle of men. "Couldn't resist me any longer, I guess." More laughter and the first lewd comments greeted this clever sally on the part of the boss's son. They clustered closer and Megan tried to shrink away from their suddenly intense stares. They made her feel considerably more unclean than the mud and grime she'd acquired during her struggle with Josh Lahood.

Unlike the permanent settlers of Carbon Canyon, all of these men were transients. They lived and worked out of the nearby bunkhouses and owed no allegiance to anyone except their employer. Many knew no other life than the daily grind of the mine. Their days consisted of endless hours spent moving rock and gravel, interrupted only by sleep, three meals, and maybe the occasional game of cards.

Some of them hadn't had a woman in more than a year, while those who had knew only the attentions of the tired slatterns who lived and worked in the cribs that fringed the bars of the larger towns. Set among such spoiled flowers, Megan Wheeler would have stood out like a rose among weeds.

"Rare up on 'er, Josh!"

"Take that cherry, son!"

"Y'all give me seconds, y'hear?"

The first speaker shoved the third. "Like hell! I'm next."

The man pushed him back. "Says who?"

"I got seniority, says who!" The two fell to fighting, giving the rest of the men something else to cheer about while adding to the spirit of violent celebration that had infused the assembly and sparking more laughter among their colleagues.

"McGill gets seconds!" Lahood was laughing as he fell down on top of the distraught Megan. "He found her. And after him," Lahood glanced meaningfully over their heads.

A sordid grin spread over Club's thick features as he saw how the wind was blowing his way. He abandoned the monitor. Left to the laws of hydraulics, the water cannon immediately went vertical, spraying into the sky like a giant fountain as its operator rushed to join the others. No one seemed to mind that it was soaking the entire camp. Logic and reason had given way to impulses uglier and more primitive.

Megan was on the verge of blacking out, but her mind somehow held together beneath the force of those obscene guffaws and leering faces. She was pounding very weakly at Josh Lahood's chest now, her tiny fists like gusts of wind on his shirt. He was using his weight to hold her in place while he worked on her with his hands. Once she'd thought of those hands as graceful. Now they were claws, ripping and tearing at her.

One hand tore her blouse from collar to waist, to the appreciative roar of the mob. All she could think of was how angry her mother was going to be at the sight of the damage. Her brain was on the verge of responding the only way it knew how: by removing her from what was taking place. She was dangerously close to going catatonic.

Something heavy and cold between her knees: Lahood's thigh, forcing her legs apart. She turned her face away. The young man was no longer handsome. His face had metamorphosed into a mask of pure evil. Better to fill her eyes with dirt than to have to stare into that mask.

Impossibly then, a sound louder than that of the fountaining monitor. The echo followed Lahood's hat as it flew off his scalp. Then the weight left her legs and belly as her assailant all but leaped to his feet. Lahood whirled, gawking first at his hat before searching out the source of the shot.

The Preacher's horse was approaching slowly, unhurriedly. The tall man astride the saddle wore his shirt open now. Of the familiar white collar there was no sign. His hat was pulled low, shading his face and hiding his eyes. Otherwise he was unchanged from the last time Lahood had seen him. He wore the same boots, mackinaw, and black shirt.

Only the empty holster that rode at his hip was new. That, and the gun in his right hand.

With the unanimous presence of mind, the circle of miners abruptly scattered in all directions like roaches at the bottom of a cracker barrel.

"Preacher!" Megan screamed. She put every ounce of strength that remained in her into the single forlorn cry. It tore

her throat, but it was unnecessary. He knew what was happening.

Startled and cheated of his pleasure, Josh Lahood's face twisted into a rictus of hate. He watched his nemesis approach warily, like a cougar that had been backed into a corner by a pack of hunting dogs. For the third time in their brief, mutually antagonistic acquaintance, the younger man's hand dropped toward his gun. Not slowly this time, not thoughtfully, but with a speed born of instinct and long practice.

He'd barely started to clear leather when something sharp struck his hand with the force of a sledge. Four quick shots followed on the heels of the first, so close upon one another that they sounded like a single impossibly long burst. It was impossible. Even if a hammer could be fanned like that, a pistol's cylinder couldn't spin that fast.

But it happened. Before it hit the ground, Lahood's pistol was struck and sent spinning, sent spinning a second time. The third time it was hit it blew up, sending metal fragments flying over the chewed-up earth. Then a fifth and last shot.

Lahood's gaze dropped to his gun hand. A round red hole had appeared in the center of it. The red stain began to spread and drip earthward. He gaped at his palm, unable to blink, shocked into silence by what had happened to him and how fast it had happened. Club stood not far away, his expression solemn. He hadn't fled along with the others, but neither did he move to intervene. He'd seen what had happened to Lahood's gun.

Now he stood there like a piece of mountain come loose, and stared thoughtfully at the intruder. There was no anger in his expression anymore. Only curiosity.

Megan struggled to her feet. She made a couple of useless,

desultory wipes at her filthy dress, then reached up with both arms, heedless of her half nudity. The Preacher leaned down from his saddle and swept her up with one arm, setting her down in front of him.

She pressed her mud-streaked face against him. Then the trembling started, and the tears came in coughing, spasming fits. He said nothing, but kept one arm tightly around her.

Then he turned his horse and they rode away, through the cloud of spray from the fountaining water cannon.

Behind them, it was very quiet for a long time.

X

"Have another one, Spider." The bartender poured the whiskey into the shot glass and looked on approvingly as the old miner drained it in two swallows. Other townsfolk crowded around the bar, casting envious glances at the nugget-filled chunk of milky quartz that rested on the hardwood and admiring ones at its inebriated but happy owner.

"Would you look at that!" one farmer was muttering.

"I wonder how many thousands it's worth?" said another.

"Over ten," ventured a self-proclaimed expert appraiser.

"Maybe twenty," argued the thin gentleman standing next to him.

Conway turned from the bar to grin at all of them. "Damn right. Twenty years o' digging pyrite out of other men's claims. Three years in that damn canyon. And I found it, me, Spider Aloyusius Conway."

He grabbed for the bottle, having to make a couple of passes at it before his fingers contacted glass. Then he straightened against the bar as he surveyed his audience. With his free hand he picked up the aggregate and then staggered forward. A rusty Patterson Colt protruded from the holster at his hip.

He nearly fell twice as he lurched out onto the main street. Despite the fog that had appeared before his face, he knew where he was heading. He'd been waiting, praying for this day for a long time and by heaven, he was going to enjoy it to the fullest.

"Hey, Spider," said a casual friend worriedly, "don't you think maybe you ought to . . . ?"

Conway didn't hear him. He heard only the voices inside his head, the ones that drove him into the middle of the street and kept him gloriously upright.

Then he was standing and staring up at the noble if spartan edifice that bore the legend LAHOOD AND SON, MINING AND SMELTING.

"Lahood! It's old Spider. Spider Conway! You remember me? You ought to, you son-of-a-bitch! Come out and tip a bottle with an honest man, you offspring of a bastard polecat! Let's see if you can stomach some square-bought whiskey."

He leaned back and tipped the bottle to his lips, letting the fiery liquid flow down his throat. It seared his belly and added to the wonderful warmth reposing there. Every drop was a delight, as much for what it represented as for how it made him feel. He was an ancient warrior and, having conquered, he was drinking the blood of his enemies.

He did not pay any special attention to the seven horses that were tied to the hitching rail in front of him.

The rest of his body might be aging rapidly, but there was

nothing wrong with his lungs. His repeated shouts had drawn the attention of the two men who occupied the office on the second-floor of the Lahood building.

Coy Lahood frowned as he set his glass of Scotch aside. The man seated on the other side of the desk rose and sauntered over to the nearest window. He looked outside for a moment, then glanced back toward the desk.

"He's calling your name, Mister Lahood."

"I know that." The magnate wore a disgusted expression as he rose and joined Stockburn in staring out the window. Together they looked down at the street and the single unsteady, taunting figure that was dancing and raving in the center of it.

"Is he one of them?" Stockburn's voice was soft and unctuous, eager to please but in no way condescending.

Lahood stared at the old sourdough cavorting drunkenly below. "Yeah. Piece of trash named Conway."

Stockburn eyed his employer curiously. "He seems to know you more than casually."

Lahood made a face. "I've had occasion to cross paths with him now and again. Aren't really that many old-timers still around. Most of 'em got smart, got religion, and got out of the way when the easy placer claims played out and the big companies started moving in. They went into carpentering or ranching and such. But there's always a few who don't know when their time is up." He nodded toward the street.

"He's one of 'em. It's too bad, you know."

"What's too bad, Mister Lahood?"

"For awhile there, I had 'em buffaloed. They were running around scared out of their boots. Couldn't wait to pack up and move out. Conway too, maybe." He shrugged.

"Well, maybe not Conway. We might've had to deal with

PALE RIDER

him even if the others had left. He's too old and too stubborn to know what's good for him anymore. Not that he would've been as much trouble as gnat piss by himself. Not with all the others gone.'' He shook his head, saddened by all the trouble he'd been forced to go to for no good reason. ''Then this damn Preacher comes along and shoots 'em full of sass.''

Stockburn's brows drew together as he looked at his employer in disbelief. ''A preacher?''

''I know it sounds ridiculous but yes, a preacher. No telling what kind of idiocy he's been stuffing those tin-pans' heads with. Whatever it was he told them, he went and got them good and riled. I told you that they turned down my offer. A thousand dollars a claim.'' The way he said it made it sound as though he still couldn't believe it.

''Seems to me, Mister Lahood, that you've gone and done just about everything a man in your position could do. Seems to me you've gone out of your way to be fair with these people. A man in your position can only do so much. You've got your reputation to think of, as well as your business.''

''Yes, that's what I told myself. Sometimes I'm too kind-hearted for my own good. So now they've gone and made me look like a fool, in addition to costing me time and money.'' He looked sharply at Stockburn. ''This Preacher. You take care of him along with the rest. He's made me look bad in front of my men. That's not good for business. Whipped three of 'em, too.''

Stockburn continued to eye him skeptically. ''A preacher did that? All by his lonesome?''

Lahood nodded curtly. ''Damned right he did. Think my men would've confessed to it if it hadn't happened?''

Stockburn considered this bit of information, then asked suspiciously, ''What's this 'preacher' look like?''

169

Lahood regarded his audience. During the converstion six other men had come into the office: Stockburn's deputies. They rarely exchanged a word even among themselves, though they responded with alacrity to the Marshal's slightest utterance. All six of them were big. None wore what could be described as a pleasant countenance. Although they were in Lahood's employ, they still made him nervous. Partly that was due to their silence, partly to the way they responded to the Marshal.

He would not have cared to encounter them without Stockburn by his side.

"To tell the truth," he finally said in response to the Marshal's question, "I never much noticed. He's tall, I guess. Six-three, maybe four. Lean but not thin. Moves smooth for a man that size. Make a good miner, though I don't think he's so inclined." He hesitated, remembering. "Something else. His eyes. For some reason I keep seeing his eyes. There's something strange about them."

Stockburn took it all in quietly. With each of Lahood's words he appeared to stand a little less at ease, to grow a bit more tense. Lahood noticed the change.

"This all mean anything to you?"

Stockburn shrugged slightly. "Maybe. Sounds like a description of a man I once knew."

"Might be. He recognized your name."

It was silent in the opulent office with only the muted soliloquy of Spider Conway to fill their ears. Lahood had heard about enough from the street. His ears were beginning to burn, and he wondered at Stockburn's hesitation.

Eventually the Marshal looked back over at him. His voice was so low that Lahood had to strain to make out the words. "Couldn't be him. The man I'm thinking about is dead."

Saying it seemed to revitalize him. He turned and strode toward the doorway. Wordlessly, his deputies filed out behind him.

Drunk as a lord, Spider Conway continued to stand in the middle of the street and bellow enthusiastically at the building in front of him. "I know you're in there, Coy!" He spat toward the building, and shook the lump of gleaming aggregate in its direction. "I got somethin' t'show ye. Come on out and have a drink, y'old sow-bellied bloat!"

Abruptly the front door was slammed open. Three of Lahood's men came out fast, as if in a hurry to escape something close on their heels. They were followed at a more decorous pace by Stockburn's deputies. The six lined up on the covered porch, three to each side of the entrance. None of them said anything to the old man in the center of the street.

Conway tried to sort out the faces through his alcohol-induced haze. He didn't recognize a one of them, though he had encountered most of Lahood's employees at one time or another. But even his whiskey-soaked brain could tell there was something different about this bunch, something different and dangerous. There was coldness in their faces that chilled him despite the liquor sloshing around in his gut.

As he stared and tried to maintain his balance, a seventh figure emerged and walked to the edge of the porch. About forty-five, Conway decided, though it was hard to tell, and not just because his senses were dulled by the whiskey. The stranger stood at the edge of the steps leading down into the street, staring back at the miner. His fingers were in constant motion, flexing and twisting.

Compared to the man standing in front of them, the six flanking the entrance were as pure as cherubim and seraphim,

Conway suddenly decided. He recoiled as if from a noxious vapor, and took a couple of uncertain steps backward.

"Where's Lahood?" The boldness the booze had given him was rapidly draining away.

"Inside," Stockburn told him. His voice was smooth, almost cloying. "Do you have a problem, old man?"

Realization finally penetrated the golden miasma that had enveloped Conway. He pointed a shaky finger at the Marshal. "I know you. You're Stockburn."

The other man laughed. "Yes, I'm Stockburn. And these," he indicated the silent men ranked behind him, "are my deputies. Maybe you've heard of them, too. Gentlemen, let's not be impolite. Say hello to Mister Conway."

Not a word came from any of the six, though one or two permitted themselves a half smile.

Spider tried to sort out his feelings, which were growing more and more confused. To help, he took another pull from the bottle. "I got no beef with you, Stockburn, or with your men. It's Coy I want to talk to."

Stockburn grinned, then spoke softly. "Well go ahead, Mister Conway." He nodded tersely toward the second-floor window. "He's right up there. He can hear you just fine."

Conway hesitated, then steeled himself and again shouted in the direction of the half-open window. "Lahood, you creepy-legged lizard, get yourself out here so's we can . . ."

His voice trailed off. His attention was drawn back to Stockburn's fingers. They still hovered at the Marshal's sides, curling and contorting in an unpredictable, snakelike dance. Conway found himself mesmerized by them.

He blinked, tottered slightly, and straightened himself. He was suddenly conscious of the fact that he was alone in the street. There were no horses, no wagons. Even the boardwalks were deserted. He was alone. The bottle he clutched and the Dutch courage it supplied no longer seemed as reassuring as they had earlier.

Within Blankenship's Emporium, Jed Blankenship glanced up from the ledger he'd been reviewing. He listened hard for a moment, then looked over at the old miner's sons. They were staring enraptured at a pair of factory-made slingshots imported from Philadelphia.

He listened to the continued silence for another minute, then addressed himself to the younger Conways. "Sounds like your daddy's running out of steam, boys. Better take him home now, huh? Don't want some rancher to run him over in the street."

"Aw, don't worry, Mister Blankenship," Eddy replied. "We only get to town once a year. Daddy's okay. He can outdrink any man this side of Placerville, he can."

"Yeah," Teddy added, "he'll be all right. He said when he was finished celebratin' he'd come get us and we'd all go over to the assay office together to get the gold out of his rock."

Blankenship shrugged and returned his attention to the ledger. It was none of his business how Conway comported himself. All he could do was suggest, and that he'd done.

Out in the street, Conway's fears were beginning to gain control over his liquor-induced bravado. The soberer he felt, the more uncomfortable he became. He was starting to see the man confronting him with greater clarity and as he did so, he was growing genuinely frightened. He swallowed nervously and looked around. There was nowhere to run to, nowhere to hide. He was all alone except for his bottle and his fortune.

Evidently Stockburn found the sourdough's transformation amusing. "I don't think Mister Lahood wants to talk to you, tin-pan. Not when you're being drunk and abusive. But maybe he'd like to watch you dance a little, hmm? Sure. That might even make up a little for some of the nasty things you've been saying about him. I think that'd be fair. Don't you, boys?'' A backward glance was rewarded with continuing silence from the line of deputies.

This nonresponse appeared to satisfy Stockburn, however. As for Conway, he knew well enough what the Marshal was talking about. A sullen gleam asserted itself in his rheumy eyes and he shook his head jerkily.

"I don't know how to dance."

"What?" Stockburn looked astonished. "An old-timer like you gone all his life without learning how to dance? Why, that's plumb unbelievable."

Before the last word was out of his mouth and in a single motion so fast as to deceive the eye, the Marshal's pistol seemed to leap into his hand of its own volition, and to fire. The slug kicked up a cloud of dust where it struck the ground two inches to the left of Conway's right boot. The old man's jump was pure reflex.

The deputies looked on impassively.

The dust settled. Conway stood there, shaking now, watching the man confronting him the way a bird watches a snake.

"There now." Stockburn's voice was as soft as ever. "I knew you must've picked up a step or two along the way. See how easy it is? You just move your feet to the rhythm."

The gun fired again, twice this time, the shots so close upon each other they sounded like one. Again Conway hopped wildly. This time the bullets struck closer to his feet.

Alarmed by the gunfire, Blankenship and the old man's sons had rushed to the boardwalk outside the store.

"God—no," the merchant whispered in horror, grasping the situation at a glance.

"Daddy!" Eddy screamed. He took a step toward the street. Alertly, Blankenship grabbed him and his brother by their collars and struggled to hold them back.

The last vestiges of drunkenness had vanished from Spider Conway's mind. He was stone-cold sober, sober enough to remember that he wasn't quite alone. He saw the movement outside the store out of the corner of his eye, and spoke without taking his gaze from Stockburn's face.

"Stay where you are, boys! No matter what happens, you stay where you are, y'hear?"

"Listen to your daddy," Blankenship urged them. He didn't release his grasp on either of them.

Stockburn idly addressed his deputies. "Some music would be appropriate, gentlemen. The show's just getting started and my hand's tired already."

Six pistols cleared leather with nary a pause between them, and began firing at one-second intervals. Under Stockburn's direction the men functioned as a single organism. One shell after another tore into the street dangerously close to Conway's boots. He tried weakly to dodge, hopping and whirling, spinning and twisting madly.

The dentist overheard the fusillade of shots and pushed his window curtains aside to peer out into the street. So did the postmistress. Slightly braver than his neighbors, the mortician cautiously poked his head out his door. He had more than a passing interest in the proceedings, which provided an excuse for his mock bravery. The majority of the citizens of Lahood, California, however, were afflicted with a sudden deafness. They remained hidden within their places of business or homes, not daring even to look outside to see what was going on.

High above, like an emperor bored with the games but conscious of their necessity, Coy Lahood sighed resignedly as he turned away from the window. What was happening below was of no more importance than a letter that needed to be answered or a repair that needed to be made to the monitor. He had better things to occupy his time with. He sat back down at his desk and began to check over the report on number-five shaft.

By now Spider was almost completely obscured by the swirling dust and the cloud of gunsmoke that enveloped him. Huffing and gasping for breath, he jerked about in a grotesque parody of his recenty victory dance in Carbon Canyon. His arms pumped wildly. Somehow he managed to hang onto both the bottle and the lump of aggregate.

Stockburn took aim through the cloud and fired twice. First the bottle disintegrated, then the lump, throwing flecks of real gold in all directions while the golden liquid splashed over Spider's pants and boots.

"Pick up the tempo, gentlemen!" Stockburn ordered his men. Wooden visaged, the line of deputies complied.

Conway was on the edge of exhaustion. His limited reserves were drained, and he'd pushed his aged frame to its limit. He could stop and risk losing a foot. He could turn and try to flee in hopes of avoiding a bullet to the back of a knee. In fact he did neither of these things because he was too tired and frightened to seriously consider them. What he did was respond in the only way a long-time survivor of the gold fields knew how: he reached for his gun.

The dust and smoke formed a wholly inadequate screen.

The gesture was seen, the response as automatic and methodical as it was predictable. All seven pistols fired simultaneously.

The slugs ripped through the lean, elderly frame from head to toe, sending blood, flesh, and fabric flying in all directions. Conway's body spun backward like a discarded rag doll and crumpled to the ground. Stockburn lifted a hand. His tone was calm as ever.

"That's enough. Thank you, gentlemen."

Blankenship could no longer restrain the two boys. They tore themselves from his restraining grasp and raced toward the motionless form lying amidst the settling dust.

The only sound was the clatter of spent shells striking the boardwalk as the deputies discarded their empty casings and calmly reloaded their weapons. Stockburn wiped his hands on his shirt, more to still their twisting than to cleanse them. He eyed the two mentally deficient youths with obvious distaste as they fell on their father's body, weeping and moaning.

Eddy's fingers touched the pool of dark blood that was seeping out from beneath the crooked, contorted frame, and lifted the stained hand mutely toward Stockburn. The Marshal recoiled as if from something vulgar.

"Take him back to Carbon Canyon," he instructed the distraught boys. "Tell this Preacher to meet me here tomorrow morning. If he doesn't, we'll come up there and find him, and while we're looking for him a few more tin-pans might get in the way."

He spun on his heel to reenter Lahood's building. The deputies filed in silently behind him, leaving the two slow-witted youths kneeling in the street, rocking and keening over their father's corpse.

*   *   *

Twilight was already creeping over the floor of Carbon Canyon. The nearly-dry steam glistened in the fading light. A few chipmunks scampered over the rocks. Squirrels gamboled in the nearby brush.

Normally none of them would have chanced a visit to the water while the sun was still up, for fear of encountering a child's rock or a miner's pistol. Squirrel stew was a popular dish among the human inhabitants of the canyon, a disquieting reality to which the small slate-gray animals had quickly become attuned. But there was no danger now. No one panned the remaining pools of shallow water or hauled buckets full to dump down quiescent Long Toms. No children stood and watched or played hide-and-seek among the boulders. The creek bottom had been abandoned to the creatures of the forest.

Smoke rose from a few rock chimneys. Up on the slope where the cabins and shanties squatted there were still hidden, furtive signs of life. But none below. No one dared to chance a trip down to the creek. The claims lay idle as their owners huddled within their pitiful shelters and tried to decide what to do next.

One man stood guard over the equipment. It was more an act of emotional than practical defiance. Ev Gossage clutched his carbine nervously, seeing a gunman behind every tree as he waited for another brace of Lahood's men to come riding into the canyon to vandalize and destroy.

A noise behind him. Something making its way through the underbrush, something much bigger than a squirrel. He whirled nervously.

A horseman was coming out of the woods on the far side of the creek, his features indistinguishable in the weak light of evening. Fearfully Gossage brought the carbine up to bear on the approaching figure, trying to keep an eye on the stranger's gun hand as well as on his face.

"S-stop! Who are you?"

The man did not respond to the warning. Gossage's trigger finger tensed. If the horseman didn't identify himself quickly, Ev knew he would have to shoot. Otherwise the man would soon be within pistol range—if he wasn't already.

Then he heard a half-remembered voice, unmistakeable in origin and tinged with amusement.

"Evening, Ev. How're the kids and the missus? You sure you know which end of that thing the bullet comes out of?"

The miner was so relieved he almost let the muzzle of the carbine drop into the mud at his feet. The tension drained out of him. On its heels came a flood of words.

"Preacher! Man, am I glad to see you! You won't believe what's happened since you've been away. Lahood set off a helluva blast at the head of the canyon and damned up the creek . . ."

The tall man's eyes flicked briefly to the nearly dried-up stream. "I guessed it was something like that."

". . . and old Spider found a peck o'nuggets in a chunk o'quartz and lit out for town with his boys. The Wheeler girl's horse come back without her, and everyone's out looking for her and her mama's goin' plumb out o' her mind with worry and we don't know the next place to look and . . ."

The Preacher had continued to approach, crossing the tiny rivulet that was all that remained of Carbon Creek, while the words continued to pour out of the miner. Now he was near enough for Gossage to make out details. The first thing he noticed was the pistol slung at the tall man's hip. The sight of the six-gun shut him up faster than any words could have. His gaze rose from the holster to the face beneath the broad-brimmed hat.

It wasn't just the presence of the gun and the corresponding absence of the starched white collar. There was something different about the man himself, Gossage decided right away. Something that had nothing to do with clothing or death-dealing appurtenances or words. It took him a moment to settle on what it was.

His manner. It was sharp and unmistakeable and apparent in the tall man's very posture. It was particularly visible in his face, though if pressed to tell, Ev Gossage couldn't have said just *what* it was that was so different. But it was there.

The Preacher leaned toward him as he rode past. "Pass the word that Megan's fine and that those still out looking for her can come back in. She just took a little spill is all."

He continued on past the gaping miner, heading for the cabins that occupied the far side of the hill. Seated behind him and until now concealed by his bulk was the slim shape of Megan Wheeler. Her hair and clothing were disheveled and she had her hands locked tightly around his waist. Gossage pushed his hat back off his forehead and stared in wonder as the pair continued on by.

"I'll be damned," he muttered.

Now what was anyone supposed to make of that?

A couple of oil lamps pushed back the night, keeping it at bay beyond the windows of the Wheeler cabin. Bess Gossage removed the flannel cozy from the bubbling teapot, then lifted the hot iron off the stove.

"Here, Sarah. Have a little of this. It's got some sassafras in it and it'll help settle your insides."

Sarah Wheeler sat despondently at the table, staring into

the flickering light of one of the lamps. Her face was drawn and her eyes were bloodshot from crying. She'd been weeping on and off all day, ever since it had been determined that her daughter was nowhere to be found in Carbon Canyon and that she had indeed gone off on Hull's mare.

She had good reason to be despondent. The number and variety of perils that existed in the wild, unforgiving mountains were uncountable. Any one of them would be sufficient to put an end to the life of a headstrong, sometimes reckless young girl.

While the sun had been out and the men had light to search by, she'd succeeded in keeping her composure. That had gone to pieces with the coming of night. Darkness would bring a forced halt to the search as well as multiplying the dangers a lone, lost girl would have to contend with. All day long Sarah had sat in the cabin, waiting for someone to cry outside, "Here she is!" Those blessed words had yet to be heard.

Now the day was all but gone, and the searchers who'd begun to trickle back to their homes before the onset of night had been unable to meet her questioning stare.

Bess Gossage would not allow herself to cry alongside her friend. That was not what Sarah needed now. She needed someone to help stiffen her resolve and relate to her fears. Bess was trying, but it wasn't easy.

"Drink up," she urged her friend and neighbor. "Ain't no good to fret. The Lord'll protect her. She's probably wanderin' around up somewheres near where she buried that pup. Gone and got herself good and turned around. Or maybe something spooked that old mare o' Hull's and it took off up a side canyon and got the both of 'em stuck. You know how Megan is about that sort o' thing. She wouldn't go and leave somebody else's property that she'd gone and borrowed.

"Probably she's sittin' around right now mutterin' and cussin' about how Hull and the rest o' the menfolk are takin' their own good time gettin' to her." She put a comforting hand on Sarah's shoulder.

"Now you drink up." She put some sugar in the cup of tea. "You got to drink somethin', even if you won't eat."

A loud crash filled the cabin and both women spun around to face the front door. It had been kicked open. The Preacher stood in the entrance, filling it for a moment before he entered. He held Megan easily in his arms.

Sarah instantly took in the filthy skirt, the torn blouse, and her eyes went to the Preacher's face. He saw the question half-hidden by the shock.

"She's all right," he told her reassuringly. "No harm done. She just needs a little rest."

He crossed to the small back bedroom and disappeared within. The movement broke Sarah's paralysis. With an inarticulate cry she bolted to catch up to him, stroking her daughter's cheek as he moved to the side of the bed, the same bed that Sarah had begun to fear would stay empty for the rest of the night and perhaps forever.

While she hovered close by, he set Megan down on the clean covers. Gently he raised the girl's head to slide the pillow beneath the long tresses. All the while she was staring up at him, at her mother, past them both at the ceiling. She did not speak. It was as if her mind were somewhere else, her thoughts borne on wings of terror and confusion to a different moment and place in time.

Discreetly, the Preacher arranged her torn blouse.

"What happened?" Sarah whispered at him, her eyes never leaving her daughter's face.

"It was Josh Lahood." The big hands moved again to adjust a bit of torn cotton. "He tried to—he tried to, but he didn't."

Megan's eyelids fluttered and her mind came back from wherever it had been. She was looking at him again, and this time she saw him.

"You're home, Megan. Everything's all right. You're back in your own room and your mother's here."

A single sob, a wrenching sound at once full of gratitude and longing, was torn from her throat. Reflexively she reached up to encircle his neck with both arms.

Sarah saw the gratitude in her daughter's eyes, but she saw the other thing that was there, too. Something as startling as it was unexpected. It made her think back to Megan's long silences of the past few days, to the distance she'd seemed to be placing between herself and her mother. Sarah had dismissed it as mere youthful, girlish moodiness. Now the real reason was revealed, and it stunned her into silence.

Stunned her, because in her daughter's face she saw mirrored her own secret hopes and longings.

She wanted to speak, to say something, but the realization of Megan's feelings numbed her. Nor was that the final shock of the evening. Now that her daughter's safety was assured, she had time to take in the collarless shirt the Preacher was wearing, and the holstered pistol slung at his side. Her eyes moved from the sobbing Megan to the tall man's face. It was a new face and yet the same, the face of a familiar stranger if such a thing were possible. Surely it was possible, for suddenly the Preacher seemed a man in which all possibilities emerged.

Hurried steps on the porch outside. They halted and were followed by Hull Barret's urgent call.

"Preacher? You in there?"

The tall man straightened and turned toward the door. As he spun his eyes locked with Sarah's for the briefest instant. In that moment he saw within the stormy conflicts, the doubts and confused desires that were playing upon her soul. Caught off guard with her innermost thoughts and feelings revealed, she turned away quickly to hide her face and the flush of embarrassment that stained her cheeks. Mercifully he said nothing, merely pushed past her to the big room beyond.

He stepped into the kitchen just as Hull came in from outside. Seeing the man he sought standing there without his turned-around collar and with a gunbelt around his waist, the miner froze. What he'd come to say came tumbling out almost absently.

"I, uh—Ev's goin' around the camp sayin' you'd brought Megan back. Is she all right?"

"She's fine, Hull. A little tired, a little scared, a little mussed up, but nothing a good night's sleep in her own bed won't cure."

The miner hesitated, still trying to make sense of the Preacher's transformation and fit it to what he had to say. Everything had happened so fast. In one day everything had changed. And now this, the most unexpected change of all.

But at least he was back. "You'd better come outside."

The tall man looked past him. "Trouble?"

Hull nodded. Together they exited the cabin, heading for the creekbed. Bess Gossage watched them leave and wondered.

The wagon had been pulled up away from the bank. The Preacher stared a long time at the torn body that lay in the buckboard's bed. His expression did not change. When he'd looked long enough, he reached out and pulled the blood-stained tarpaulin back down to cover the motionless form.

Eddy Conway forced back his tears as best he was able

while he tried to explain. "Then him and his men, they shot him. They kept shooting him, it seemed like. Over and over. The bullets kept hitting him forever." His voice trailed off into the night.

"Why'd they do that?" His brother was mumbling to himself more than to the assembled group of miners. He was staring brokenly at the tarp. "Why'd they have to do that? He wasn't hurtin' nothin'. Daddy never hurt nobody in his life. Why? Why why why?"

The silent men had no answer for the simple Teddy. The search for Sarah Wheeler's missing daughter had exhausted them. This new tragedy had numbed them into silence.

Up until now Lahood had done no more than harry and bedevil them, killing chickens, dirtying laundry, and breaking up their equipment. Many times it had seemed no worse than a wearying, burdensome game. Spider's corpse was indication enough that their nemesis was through playing. There would be no more games.

Conway had been in Carbon Canyon longer than any of them. He was the one who'd found the first color, who'd determined that the creek had more to offer the persistent than just dust, who'd welcomed each newcomer with a gruff greeting, inviting them to try their luck. He hadn't begrudged the new arrivals their claims or their occasional discoveries, seeming to take as much pleasure in another man's find as he did in his own. Conway had been indestructible, as solid as the surrounding mountains.

Now he was dead, shot to pieces by cold, uncaring strangers Lahood had brought in to put an end once and for all to his argument with the settlers of Carbon Canyon.

"It was him, wasn't it?" Ev Gossage looked up at the Preacher. "The Marshal you warned us about?"

The tall man turned away from the wagon to stare downstream. "Yeah. Stockburn. Stockburn and his deputies. I figured him to be here about now. That's the way Lahood would want to work it." He glanced back toward the wagon and its sad, solitary load. "What I didn't figure was for Spider to go riding off into town to get drunk."

Teddy looked from his father's body to the Preacher. "He said—the Marshal said to tell the Preacher to come to town in the morning. He said for you to come or else he and his men would come up here lookin' for you."

Silence. Hull frowned at his friend. "I don't figure it. Why you? It's our claims he wants."

All eyes focused on the stranger in their midst, on the man who had returned to them wearing a six-gun instead of the collar. They began to drift away, distancing themselves from him. It was as if he carried some dangerous disease, and it was prudent to distance yourself from a sick man, whether he was your friend or not. The symbol of the disease was the gun that hung at his hip.

It had nothing to do with personal feelings of friendship. The presence of the gun changed things even more than did the absence of the collar. Only Hull Barret stayed close. Barret—and Conway. No longer would they have the old man's cagy defiance to inspire them to resist.

"That night, the night you warned us about this Stockburn, it sounded almost like you knew him." Jake Henderson's voice was hushed. "Spider asked you that hisself. Is it true?"

Everyone waited for the Preacher's reply. He let his gaze sweep over the group, touching each man individually, and all who were so touched remembered it forever afterward.

"The vote you took the other night showed courage. You voted to stick together. That's what you've got to do. I don't have anything to do with that. You've built something in this place that's worth fighting for, but you've got to decide that for yourselves, and you've got to be ready to defend what you've made with something besides words.

"Spider went in alone. That was his mistake. He went in drunk, which is worse. Something all of you'd better learn good, and you'd better learn now: only by standing together can you beat the Lahoods of this world. Whatever happens tomorrow, never forget that. If you do, you're lost. You might as well sign your souls over now to any man that'll pay you for 'em." He turned his gaze on the still form outlined by the tarp.

"You've got a brave man there. He deserves a proper burial. You all know how to use a shovel. You'd best get on with it."

An uncertain voice piped up from the back of the crowd. "Preacher, we ain't got no proper cemetery here."

"There's others buried in this canyon, ain't there?"

"Well, yeah."

"It's a man who makes the ground hallowed, not the other way around. He died for this place. It's fitting he be buried here." The tall man turned away and started to head upslope.

"Preacher?" Ev Gossage spoke a little too quickly. The tall man paused and turned to face him. The miner looked to his neighbors for support but that did little to alleviate the uncomfortable knot in the pit of his stomach. "You *are* goin' into town tomorrow, ain't you?"

The Preacher gazed back down at him for a long moment. Then he spun on his heel and strode off into the darkness without replying. Hull Barret whirled angrily on his friend.

"How can you *say* that, Ev? Didn't you hear a word of

187

what he just said?" He looked past Gossage, at his other neighbors. "didn't any of you hear what he just said?"

No one replied and none of them would meet his eyes. They began to drift away, singly at first, then in twos and threes, skulking off into the darkness in the direction of their homes.

But the night couldn't protect them from their own fears, and their minds would not let them escape from their own burning embarrassment.

XI

He wanted to be alone, despite Hull's protestations that he was still welcome in his cabin. Nothing against Hull's hospitality, he explained. He just wanted to be alone.

So they put him up in Ulrik Lindquist's old place. He sat at the table sliding cartridges into the .44 one at a time, checking each one carefully. The golden light of the oil lamp was turned up all the way, the wick riding high in its holder. The coffee pot Hull had provided steamed away on the stove behind him.

There was a creak from the front porch. The door was opened from outside. It let in the cold night air and the shawl-wrapped figure of Sarah Wheeler. She stood there for a moment, looking at him. Then she closed the door behind her.

He turned his attention back to his work. In the soft light the pistol took on a glow of its own, the blued steel seeming to produce its own internal illumination. He spoke without looking up at her.

"Megan feeling any better?"

"She's sleeping. She cried herself to sleep. I cleaned her up as best I could. Better just to leave her alone for awhile. I wanted—I wanted to come and thank you for what you did. Megan's all I've got. Sometimes I forget that. Living in a place like this can make you forget what's really important. Thank you for bringing her back to me."

"No need for the extra thanks. I'm just glad I happened by."

She watched him silently as he manipulated the engine of death. First he methodically loaded the remaining chambers, then he picked up a soiled rag and ran it over every part of the weapon, refining the already awesome shine. He held the pistol easily, handling it with a quiet familiarity that frightened her. His neck looked naked without the white collar to hide it from view.

There was so much happening inside her that she didn't know how to deal with, so much she needed to say that she couldn't put into words. She moved toward the table until she was standing very close to him.

"That first day, when Hull told me what you'd done in town, I knew you were a gunfighter."

He half smiled. "Really? Now how did you know that?"

"Nobody in this country goes up against three men without a gun to back him up."

"They don't?"

"Don't tease me." She nodded curtly at the well-worn .44. "What about that?"

"Lots of people carry guns. That doesn't make them all gunfighters."

She mulled that over before replying. "Megan told me what you did to Josh Lahood. Right there in the middle of his camp, in front of all his men. Who but a gunfighter could do such a thing and get away with it?"

"Seems to me I recall something about another fellow a long time ago who went up against a bunch of soldiers without much caring what might happen to him."

"Yes, and look what did happen to him."

There was silence for awhile. He made a final check of the gun, shut the cylinder with a click. Then he nodded toward the steaming coffee pot. "Cold out tonight. Want some coffee?"

She didn't move, couldn't speak. The cabin was not air tight and a gentle breeze pressed in from around the door, ruffling her hair. Finally, "There's a lot of talk going around. Everyone's sayin' you're going into town to face that Marshal and his deputies. By yourself."

He slid the pistol into the holster that rested on the table. "Is that what they're saying?"

"Is it true?"

"Yeah."

"Don't. Please."

He shrugged. "It's an old score. There's more to it than the problems of the folks in Carbon Canyon. Time's come to settle things. Could've come some time before now, could've come later. Could've been some other place. It just happens to be here and now. That's the way it's got to be. I can't help that."

"Isn't there anything I could say, or do, to change your mind?"

Something in the way she said it made him look sharply up at her. He rose from the table, went to the stove, and poured two cups of coffee. She kept her back to him, unable to look him in the face as she spoke. The words she'd been trying to say every day since he'd arrived came pouring out.

"When you left the other day without saying anything, without telling anyone, it reminded me of the other time someone left me. Left me in the same way. After that I swore I'd never let myself be hurt again because I'd never love again.

"Then you rode into Carbon Canyon, and into our lives, and I couldn't help the way I felt." Her hands balled into tiny fists. "God, if only I could control the way I feel!" She inhaled deeply.

"When you left like that I thought sure you'd gone forever. It forced me to reassess what I'd been thinking, to look at things in a new light. Sometimes you need something like that to make you appreciate what you have instead of mooning over what you want but can never have. I need a man who'll never leave me again, who'll stay at my side for the rest of my days. If I married again and he ran out on me it would kill me as sure as one of Stockburn's bullets. Can you understand that?"

He set the coffee pot back on the stove. "Yes. It's not so very complicated, you know."

She nodded. "And you'd have left again one day, wouldn't you?"

A long pause, then, "Yes."

She shut her eyes tight, then opened them again. She sounded almost grateful. "I thought as much. Then this way is best. Best all around. I'm going to marry Hull."

"I think that's a fine idea," he said evenly. "Hull's a good man. He'll make a fine husband."

"I never doubted it. I just was never completely certain

before—before now. Now I'm sure." She turned and walked over to him. He turned to face her. She could handle that now, she was pleased to discover. It wasn't so difficult, now that she was ready to face everything else.

But there was one more thing she had to do to make sure within herself, to make it final.

"This is just so I won't have to wake up at night for the rest of my life, wondering..."

Rising on tiptoes, she put her arms around his neck and kissed him. He did not resist, but neither was there the response she both hoped for and feared. She released him, turned, and headed for the door.

"Goodbye," she said softly as she opened it.

"Goodbye, Sarah."

She stepped outside—and froze. It was the sound that stopped her cold, not the chill of night. It came floating down the canyon, echoing off the granite walls, a faint but comprehensible wail. A single word, long and drawn out. It did not sound entirely human.

"*Preeeaccchherrrr!*"

Sarah stood staring fearfully out into the darkness as the eerie, ephemeral call faded away.

"Close the door," the Preacher told her. "Mosquitoes'll get in."

"It's too cold for mosquitoes." But she retreated and shut the heavy oak barrier behind her. "Who is it?"

They heard it again, a high, keening moan that cried out for a response.

"*Preeeaccchherrrr!*"

The wick in the lamp had been burning high. The oil had been exhausted. Now the light sputtered and died. The tall man and Sarah stood close to each other in the darkened room. Moonlight flooded in through the windows.

She stared at his half-hidden face, trying to penetrate the veil of mystery in which he'd cloaked himself ever since he'd come among them. In some ways the moonlight was more revealing than the bright light of day. It threw everything into sharp relief: his features, his expression, that unblinking stare.

What did they know about him, really? Not where he came from, not where he'd been going when he'd stumbled by accident into their tense little community. What did he really want with them? Was there some deeper purpose behind his actions, or was he truly just responding to events as they developed?

"Who are you?" she murmured. "Who are you, really?"

He smiled gently down at her. "It doesn't really matter, does it? Not now."

He was right. It didn't. Events had been set in motion. They would move to a conclusion of their own momentum. Whatever happened now was out of their hands. They could no more change what was going to happen tomorrow than they could alter the inclination of the Earth.

"*Prreeaccheerrrr!*"

That inhuman howl again, hopefully for the last time, Sarah thought. This time there was an undercurrent of frustration and uncertainty to it. She moved a little closer to the tall man.

One by one, as if to ward off the spell the cry cast over them, the inhabitants of Carbon Canyon extinguished their fires and their lamps. Within their shacks and shanties they huddled together for warmth and reassurance. Death stalked the morrow, and each man prayed that it would not visit him or his family. And as they prayed, they tried hard to convince themselves it was common sense that ruled their actions rather than cowardice.

The Preacher rose with the sun. There was much to do and no time to waste in getting it done, but he still took the time to observe the civilized amenities. Wash and shave, then a brief breakfast of hard bread and a little bacon. A final check of gun and shells, then one last task to perform before he set out.

He'd checked the heavy wooden box earlier and was familiar with its contents. Now he carried it outside onto the porch and broke the seal with his knife, kicking the lid aside. The half-foot-long red cylinders the box contained were stacked neatly within the inner padding.

His horse waited patiently as he began filling one saddlebag with the dynamite. Then he added coils of fuse, more than he was likely to need. Each fuse would have to be short and burn fast. When the box was half empty, he slung the saddlebags over the gelding's withers, took a last look at the empty cabin, and climbed into the saddle. Mackinaw and bedroll formed a tightly wrapped bundle behind the cantle.

A fine, warm day. The Sierras' farewell to summer, a salutary prelude to the onrushing November. But he wouldn't need the mackinaw today. He would not have had it on if it had been twenty degrees colder. He was going to have to be able to move as quickly as possible.

He started away from the cabin and had gone no more than a few yards when the flash of light on metal made him halt. His fingers dipped toward the holstered .44, then relaxed.

Hull came out from behind the cabin on his well-rested mare and grinned at him. It was apparent he'd been waiting back there for some time. An old Sharps .59-90 lay across his legs.

The Preacher eyed him quizzically. "Morning, Barret. Little early for you, isn't it?"

"A little," Hull agreed. He looked heavenward. "Nice day to be out, though. Too nice for sleepin' in. I see you're of the same mind."

"Affairs that need attending to." The tall man nodded at the oversized rifle. "Quite a hunk of iron. Good for driving nails or hunting buffalo. Problem is, there ain't any hereabouts. You plan on using that thing for what it was designed for, you need to be about a thousand miles east of here."

"Depends on what you're hunting. Besides, it's too nice a day to be out ridin' alone. I'm goin' with you."

The Preacher stared hard at his friend. Hull was nervous, that was clear enough for anyone to see. He was also determined.

"No buffalo where I'm going, neither."

"I know." The miner shifted the position of the huge rifle so that the barrel pointed, as if coincidentally, at his companion. It was an impressive old weapon, but bulky. Hard to bring to bear in a hurry, and a single-shot to boot.

"Even with that cannon, you wouldn't stand a chance."

The other man showed no indication of being ready to back down. "That's for me to decide, ain't it?"

There was a long pause. The Preacher's eyes burned into Hull's. The miner met that unsparing gaze without flinching or turning away. Eventually the tall man shrugged.

"Suit yourself."

He flicked the reins, and his horse started forward at a canter. Hull's mare fell in alongside. Neither man spoke. There was no need. Everything that had to be said had been said.

*   *   *

The sun was still rising over the walls of Cobalt Canyon. The bunkhouse door was still closed against the cold night air. From the cookhouse smoke was rising, along with the sharp odors of frying bacon and fresh bread. Soon the men would come staggering out. In less than an hour, every one of them would be hard at work.

The machinery slept along with the men. The monitor hung slack in its gymbal, its power held in check, waiting for men to lift its nozzle to the still unblemished hillside across the creekbed, waiting for others to fill it with the power of Cobalt Creek.

Somewhere a Stellar jay chirped, heralding the arrival of the sun. It let out a startled squawk and flew off as a red and orange flower erupted from the base of the monitor platform, to be followed instantly by a numbing earth-shaking blast. The platform exploded in a geyser of splinters. The monitor teetered drunkenly atop it for a moment before tumbling heavily to the ground. Metal bent and rivets popped free as the water cannon smashed against the boulders below.

Moving as fast as possible over the slippery, uneven terrain, the Preacher's gelding came flying through the dust of the explosion. A long cigar was clamped tightly between the horseman's teeth. A pair of red tubes in his right hand, he galloped straight for the forty-foot-long iron sluice that was used to divert the creek's flow. Each tube flicked the tip of the burning cigar and began to hiss and sputter. He dropped them as he rode on beneath the sluice.

Two more explosions followed his passage, each close upon the other, lifting the body of the sluice off the ground. Fragments of it flew into the dry streambed and *whanged* off rocks, sending sparks flying.

At the same time Hull Barret was circling the main toolshed. He tossed a stick of dynamite against the base of the building, then put one hand on his hat to hold it in place as he rode like hell for somewheres else. The Preacher had cut the fuses breathtakingly short and there was no time to hang around and enjoy the show.

The echo of the explosion mixed with those the Preacher had already set off. Multiple reverberations caromed through one another as they bounced off the flanks of the canyon. The toolshed came apart like a matchbox, sending nails and picks and bits of shattered lumber flying in all directions.

The bunkhouse door was slammed open. Club stood there, clad in mangy oversized longjohns. He had barely enough time to take in the ruined monitor platform, the devastated sluice, and the concrete slab that had once formed a foundation for the toolshed before his eyes widened in horror at the specter that stood not ten yards in front of him.

It was the Preacher. He sat easily astride his horse, holding a fulminating stick of dynamite in one hand. He did not move to throw it. Instead he just held it firmly, as though the fast-shrinking fuse was of no concern to him, and stared significantly back at the giant.

Club was neither an intellectual nor an idiot, and he grasped the import of the Preacher's position instantly. He ducked back inside the bunkhouse to shout a warning. In seconds the door was filled with half-naked, half-asleep roughnecks scrambling for cover.

As soon as the last man was out the Preacher tossed the dynamite inside. There was less than half an inch of fuse left. Turning his mount quickly, he sent it sprinting down the canyon. As he rode past Club's position he found time to proffer a casual salute. The giant grinned back at him and returned the gesture. Then he joined the rest of the miners in an exercise known as digging for gold without pick or shovel.

Seconds later there was dirt in his mouth and heat on his back as the bunkhouse erupted, throwing skyward a mass of wood, clothing, and assorted personal possessions. Something bounced off the giant's back and came to rest in front of his face. A broken shaving mug. He eyed it thoughtfully from his prone position. Somehow he didn't think it would be prudent to rise and expose himself just yet.

In this Club demonstrated unsuspected wisdom, because Hull and the Preacher had not yet concluded their visit. They continued to ride through the camp, seeking out suitable subjects for attention until they had expended the last of the dynamite. Explosion upon explosion rent the air, until not a single structure remained standing. The canyon was filled with dust that would be a long time in settling.

Under this cover the two men made their escape, climbing an old trail into the woods that lined the south ridge. There they paused to survey their handiwork. Flames danced within the ruins of the bunkhouse, and there would be no breakfast served in the cookhouse this morning, or any morning soon after. They could make out the more intrepid among the roughnecks beginning to pick their way through the camp, trying to salvage what they could. There was no sign of anyone attempting to mount a counterattack. Nor was there likely to be any. Among the casualties of the ride-through was the camp's corral, whose four-legged occupants, spurred to ragged flight by the repeated explosions, should be halfway to Sacramento by now.

Still, there was one stick of dynamite left. The Preacher lit it, watched it sputter, and drew back his hand to let fly this final farewell in the direction of the camp below—only to have the hissing charge slip from his grasp. It rolled right under Hull's mare.

"Uh-oh," the tall man murmured.

Eyes wide, Hull vaulted from his saddle, picked up the stick, and hurled it over the side of the ridge. The resultant explosion sent the shell-shocked miners below racing frantically for their cover as dirt and brush fountained skyward.

Even as the explosive went off, the Preacher was leaning over to smack the riderless mare sharply on her rump. She immediately bolted up the hill. Barret whirled to gaze up at his friend in surprise.

"What the hell?"

The tall horseman grinned down at him even as he spurred his own mount forward. "You're a good man, Barret. I envy you your future. Take care of Sarah and the girl."

"Hey, wait a minute, you can't—!"

But of course he could, because he was already riding for the far slope, leaving Hull staring helplessly after him. Hull considered his own position. Eventually his own horse would stop running (on the other side of the ridge, most likely) and would halt to crop the fresh mountain grass, wondering why it had been aimlessly charging through the woods in the first place. But by that time it would be afternoon, and by the time he could get into town it would be too late to help with anything.

He had been well and truly (if fondly) snookered, and there wasn't a damn thing he could do about it. His first reaction was anger. That changed when he had time to think, when he realized what had been done to him and why. He raised a hand to wave as the distant horseman topped the far ridge.

"So long—Preacher." Then he turned and started off in the direction his wayward mount had taken.

*   *   *

The sun was bright and warm on the front of the cabin. It was almost comfortable inside when Megan emerged from her bedroom. She was fully dressed and running a brush through her hair. She'd washed it four times this morning, but she still didn't feel completely clean.

Her mother was working over the stove, finalizing preparations for breakfast. It took a moment before she noted her daughter's presence. When she did, there was a hint of surprise in her voice.

"I thought you were still asleep." She inspected her daughter's attire. "Very pretty. That's not like you unless you're going someplace."

"I'm not going anywhere," Megan replied softly. She turned to look out the window, still running the boar bristles through her long hair. "The Preacher's gone, isn't he?"

Taken aback, Sarah turned her attention back to the bacon and eggs that were sizzling in the cast-iron skillet. "Yes. Last night."

Megan pivoted to stare unswervingly at her mother. "Did you tell him you loved him?"

Sarah hesitated momentarily while she searched for a reply that would be safe as well as truthful. "He knows we both love him."

The younger woman considered this, then nodded approvingly. "I understand. Did you say goodbye to him?"

"Yes."

Another nod. Then Megan turned back to the door. Her expression was solemn, and very grown-up. "I didn't. I'm sorry for that."

She opened the door and went out onto the porch. Her mother gazed after her for a long minute. Then she turned away. It was a new morning and she didn't want to burn their breakfast.

Idly she wondered where Hull had got himself to. It wasn't like him to miss breakfast.

XII

It was a fine day, bright and sunny, and all was right with the world as far as Lahood's foreman was concerned. McGill was relaxing in one of the chairs that sat on the porch fronting the Lahood building. Jagou and Tyson were there with him, along with a couple of the other boys. The troubles of the past week were history now. There was nothing more to worry about. Not since Stockburn and his men had come aboard.

McGill had been assured that by the end of the week they would be moving equipment and supplies from Cobalt Canyon over to Carbon. Then the profits and concommitant bonuses would really begin to flow, according to the Boss.

A few townies were walking up and down the boardwalks, intent on their own business. It was late in the morning and the streets were largely deserted. Most of the men in this part of the world were already hard at work. McGill and his men would be joining them soon, running a wagonload of supplies up to the camp.

He squinted suddenly, then wiped at his eyes. The sun was playing tricks with him, sucking up illusions out of the dust and dirt. Except that it was too precise, too sharp to be an illusion.

"I'll be damned," he muttered. He kicked forward, rising from the chair. His men eyed him apprehensively, wondering at the unexpectedly abrupt movement, until one by one they also saw what he was staring at.

McGill was gazing at the far end of Main Street. A single horseman had rounded the corner and was approaching. His animal's pace was measured and unhurried.

The barber saw him next. He gaped out the window as the tall stranger trotted past. Then he quickly drew his curtains. The postmistress also noted the stranger's passage and rushed to bolt the post office door. Anyone wanting to purchase stamps was in for a long wait.

Only the town's mortician appeared unaffected, though he took care to fasten the shutters that protected his windows. Stained glass was expensive and difficult to come by in Gold Rush country, and men about to engage in serious discussion historically had little regard for private property.

Lahood received the message quietly, dismissed the man who'd brought it. Then he rose from his desk, turned, and walked over to the window that looked out onto the street. The Marshal accompanied him. Lahood held the curtain aside and together they observed the approach of the solitary horseman.

"That's him," Lahood muttered. "That's the one they call the Preacher, all right."

Stockburn was less than fascinated, though he stared intently at the tall rider. "Uh-huh."

"Ever see him before?"

The Marshal bent low, but the rider's face remained hidden by the broad brim of his hat. "Can't see too well from here."

They continued to stare as the rider brought his horse to a halt outside Blankenship's emporium. Casually the stranger

ismounted and tethered his animal. Then he strolled inside.
He hadn't so much as glanced in the direction of the five
hostile men who were eyeing him from across the street.

The Preacher surveyed the interior of the store, assuring
himself no other customers were present. Then he strode
toward the small dining area, passing the place where the
proprietor was hard at work on his ledgers.

"Morning, Blankenship." The greeting was offered in
passing and he did not look at the owner when he spoke, but
he was the recipient of a long stare by way of reply.

The merchant knew who his visitor was. He remembered
the first time he'd come into the store several days previous.
A lot had happened in the county since then, most of it
evolving in one way or another around this man. Blankenship
wondered what was going to happen next.

The Preacher slipped onto a stool opposite the lunch
counter and smiled warmly at the woman on the other side.
She turned from her pots and casseroles to serve him.

"Morning, ma'am."

"Morning, son. Coffee?" He nodded, and she poured a
steaming cupful from the pot that had been simmering on the
stove.

"Thanks." He hefted the cup and sipped at the steaming
brew. It was good and hot, and it felt just right as it burned
his throat and settled in his gut. He glanced over the top of
the cup toward the street outside, set the half-emptied cup
back down on the counter.

"Nice day," said Mrs. Blankenship conversationally. When
he didn't reply, she let her own gaze drift toward the window,
and she saw the five men chatting animatedly on the porch of
the Lahood building. Occasionally one would pause to point
across the street. Then two or three hard stares would echo

the gesture. There was concern in her voice when she spok
again.

"Hate to see so nice a day spoiled before it's had a chanc
to get started."

"Sometimes it can't be helped."

She nodded somberly. "More coffee?"

He held out the cup. "Thanks." He sipped at it, eyeing h
over the porcelain rim. "Since it's such a nice day, it mig
be a good idea if you and your husband took a little walk

She nodded again, then turned from him to wipe her hand
As he worked on the rest of his coffee she began putting h
cookware and crockery in order with more than usual spee

One of the five men broke away from the others to scutt
across the street. He ran low and hunched over, bobbing a
weaving, while his companions anxiously followed his prog
ress. Reaching the far side, Jagou rose slowly until he cou
just see into the general store. What he saw made his eyes
wide.

Ducking down again, he retraced his circuitous course ba
across the street to rejoin his cronies.

"Well, what's he doin'?" McGill demanded to know.

"Yeah, where's he at?" added a concerned Tyson.

Jagou replied in a baffled whisper. "Damndest thing y
ever saw. The big sonofabitch is just sittin' there drinki
coffee. Even got his back to the door."

The five exchanged looks. McGill licked his lips thoug
fully as he eyed the store opposite. "Well, what do y
think? What about it?"

"Boss'd sure be grateful," Tyson ventured.

"Yeah," said one of the other men. "Bet he'd give u
week off in Sacramento."

"Maybe two." Jagou's eyes were shining now. "With ay."

"Then what the hell are we sittin' here for?" Tyson ondered. "McGill?"

The foreman considered. There was still no sign of move-ent from the store across the street, but he knew the reacher wouldn't sit there drinking coffee forever. Every-ing about the bonuses and the time off the men had been lking about was reasonable. Lahood could be a hard driver, it he never failed to reward a man for a job well done.

Hadn't he once told McGill personally that the most suc-ssful men used their own initiative?

The temptation was too great, the potential rewards too ear, for anyone to pass up. "Well, I reckon the five of us n't need the Marshal, do we?"

Ready agreement came from his men. Chairs were shoved ide. Hands dropped to make certain of the location of stols.

They crossed the street one at a time so as not to draw tention to themselves. Each man moved fast and stayed low. lready they could feel the gold that Lahood was going to vish on them. They regrouped outside Blankenship's, guns awn. McGill checked to make sure each man was ready. hen he brought his raised arm down sharply.

They burst through the doorway with every gun firing. andy jars exploded along with their colorful contents as ells ripped through the transparent cylinders. Mrs. Blanken-ip's kitchen was laid waste as milk, soup, and coffee lattered the walls. Pots and utensils were riddled with les, mugs and dishes blown to shards. Even the pickle barrel me apart as its staves were sliced by flying slugs. Brine and

pickles flooded the floor of the emporium in a green ti
wave.

Stockburn and Lahood had rushed back to the window
the first sound of the attack. They stared across the street
the fusillade continued without let-up. Lahood looked relieve

"Well, Marshal, it appears you won't have to both
yourself with the Preacher. Frankly I didn't give McC
credit for that much forethought. I guess he decided he a
his boys could handle this themselves. You'll still receive
agreed-upon contingency fee, of course."

Stockburn's expression had not changed, nor did he app
to be paying much attention to the magnate's words.
continued to peer through the window at the street outsid

"We'll see," he finally murmured. "It isn't over yet."

Lahood smiled condescendingly. "McGill isn't too brig
but he's thorough. That's why I made him my foreman. I l
a man who's sure of his work and doesn't take chances.'

Stockburn had nothing more to say.

Within the emporium, McGill and his men were runn
out of targets and shells. It was impossible to see anyth
through the boiling cloud of gunsmoke. Without having to
ordered to, the men finally stopped shooting. Through
slowly dispersing smoke it became possible to pick out
ruins of the store, now decorated with broken glass a
cartons. Underfoot was a slippery, slimy blend of varicolo
liquids.

They could see everything, in fact, except a body.

Tyson and Jagou looked bewildered as they waved av
the clinging smoke. McGill moved forward, trying to p
behind the counter without exposing any more of himself t
was absolutely necessary. He was here somewhere, ly
behind something, riddled with their bullets. The slugs

st knocked him backward somewhere out of sight, that was
. They'd find him in a minute or so.

He was right about the last.

"Looking for someone?" a calm voice inquired.

They turned in unison, eyes widening in fear, their legs
rning to jelly. Guns started to swing up and around.

Lahood and Stockburn listened intently as the gunfire
side the store was suddenly and unexpectedly resumed. It
dn't last half as long as the first exchange, nor did it fade
ay gradually as it had previously. A last shot rang out,
en—silence.

Several minutes passed. A single figure emerged from the
nt of the store. It looked briefly up at the Lahood building,
en turned up the boardwalk. The tall man moved at a
surely pace with long, unhurried strides.

A good deal of Lahood's carefully cultivated air of *savoir
re* vanished. His jaw dropped as he followed the tall man's
ogress.

"Jesus! What the hell's he doing *now*?"

As they stared, the Preacher suddenly stepped out into the
eet. At first Lahood thought he was going to cross over.
stead, he stopped in the center of the avenue, turned south,
d began reloading his pistol.

Stockburn's expression was set. He straightened and let the
rtain fall back into place. "He's inviting us to join him."

"He's insane." Lahood was unable to believe what he was
eing, just as he was unable to accept the Marshal's explana-
n. "The man is plumb loco. Isn't he? Stockburn?" He
ned from the window.

The Marshal was gone. The door to the office stood open.
ter a moment's thought, Lahood closed it, then returned to
ume his vigil at the window. There was nothing to worry

about, nothing at all. Stockburn and his men would finish t
and he could get back to business.

But if he wasn't worried, then why was he sudde
perspiring so heavily? Crazy—that damn fool McGill! T
man didn't have enough upstairs. He'd been a willing enou
worker, but then so was a good dog. Went in without a pl
without checking out the lay of the land. Too bad for hi
then. He should've held off and let the professionals do
job. That's what came of letting amateurs strike out on th
own.

No, there was nothing to worry about at all.

The door to the Lahood building opened. Stockbur
deputies emerged and arranged themselves with ritual pre
sion. Three to the right side of the doorway, three to the l
Finally Stockburn came out and turned his gaze up the stre

As the Marshal appeared the Preacher slid home the
cartridge. He snapped the .44's cylinder shut and slid the
gun back into its holster. Standing there by himself in
middle of Main Street, he hardly seemed to be breathing. T
distance that separated him from Stockburn and the depu
was not great. The sun was high, eliminating shadows a
warming him.

He waited.

Stockburn's men gazed back at their quarry. There was
cover in the middle of the street, nothing to duck behind,
place to run. They considered this aspect of their
dispassionately, as they did with every other job. They did
think of their opposition as gallant or brave. Nor did t
regard him as foolhardy or particularly stupid. To them
was nothing more than a cipher, a time card to be punch
something to be resolved as quickly and efficiently as po

e. That was why they were in Stockburn's employ. That is what they would do.

As if marching in time to some unheard rhythm, they descended from the porch and crossed into the street. They stared at the single figure confronting them as they formed a single line stretching from boardwalk to boardwalk. His hand moved ever so slightly nearer the staghorn grip of his pistol. Stockburn nodded slightly, and the line began to advance. Beneath the shading brim of his hat, the Preacher's eyes narrowed. He moved to meet them.

As they always did at such moments the Marshal's fingers began to twitch, curling and twisting about themselves where they hung suspended above the handle of his gun. His attention was fixed on the single man walking toward him, searching for some sign of weakness or any movement toward the oversized .44. He was also straining to make out the features staring back at him, but the wide-brimmed hat held them in shadow.

The distance between the one and the seven closed. To forty-five yards, then to thirty, twenty-five . . .

At twenty-three yards the deputy on the far right went for his gun. The Preacher reacted immediately, and Stockburn and his men reacted to that. The air was filled with swirling black smoke and the thunder of eight pistols firing as rapidly as possible.

When the forty-eighth shell had been spent, the firing stopped. The haze began to dissipate.

Three of Stockburn's men lay dead on the ground. Opposite them, lying motionless in the dust was—a broad-brimmed hat. There were two holes in it, one in the crown, one along the left edge. Of its owner there was no sign.

Stockburn's smile was cynical and knowledgeable. He

barely glanced at the three corpses as he hastened to reloa
His eyes flickered over the buildings that lined both sides
the street.

"Fan out," he said tersely. "Find him."

Without a word, the three surviving deputies split
reloading as they ran.

A preternatural silence had engulfed the town, as thoug
had been afflicted with the plague. Nothing moved on
streets or within the silent buildings. The inhabitants
Lahood, California, had retreated to their bedrooms and in
sanctums. They would huddle there, trying to pretend t
nothing was happening within earshot of their comforta
little lives, shutting out the knowledge of what was tak
place in their streets, until the sound and fury went away
its own accord.

One of the deputies had rushed up to the hat that lay in
street. Standing over it, he glanced sharply to this right, t
turned to race down a narrow alley that separated a pair
two-story buildings. It was the most logical escape route
their quarry to have taken. Holding his pistol at the ready,
began checking windows and doorways, barrels and po
ready to fire at the slightest suggestion of movement.

Ahead was a door into the building on his right. It st
half open. As the deputy stared it moved slightly on
hinges, as if nudged by a gentle breeze. But there was
wind. The midday air was still as death.

The deputy's expression did not change as his eyes faste
on the doorway. Taking one long jump to his left, he lan
in a crouching position even as he began to fan the hamm
on his gun, emptying the contents of the cylinder into
door. The wood was particularly thick. It recoiled under

impact of the heavy slugs. Then it began to come apart, its center section chest-high blown to bits by the six shells.

The deputy reloaded rapidly, then advanced on the blasted door. Pushing it inward with his right boot, he paused a moment to listen to the silence. Then he stepped through the portal.

The single shot that greeted this entrance was loud in the confines of the hallway. A look of profound surprise came over the deputy's face as a hole appeared in his forehead. He kept that look as he toppled over backward.

Stockburn heard the single shot that followed close on the heels of the volley of six. He glanced sharply to his right. Then he began to move.

Deputy Kobold came racing around the back end of the alley, but pulled up fast when he saw his colleague's body lying sprawled in the dirt. Cautiously he peered around the corner.

There was a huge livery stable across the small side street where the alley ended. Its back bay doors were standing open. The deputy was just in time to see a tall shape disappear inside. The man did not look back and so did not see his stalker. A pleased grin spread across the deputy's face. Noiselessly he ran toward the double doors.

He slowed as he reached the stable, glanced inside, and pulled his head back. His brief exposure drew no reaction from within. Nor was there any activity when he darted into the shadowed interior. He kept his back pressed against an exterior wall as he scanned the cavernous structure.

Thin rays of light poured through cracks in the roof. Horses munched contentedly in their stalls. Tresses of alfalfa streamed from the storage lofts overhead. Nearby was a three-walled alcove filled with saddlery and other gear. Something within the tack room caught the deputy's eye. He darted toward it, keeping low and watching possible hiding places.

On a shelf within was a shotgun. It was old, but well maintained and freshly oiled. It hardly made a sound as Kobold broke back the breech and slid a shell into each barrel. He snapped it shut and drew back both hammers.

Stepping out into the vaulted main chamber, he began to saturate the livery stable. Horses pitched and screamed, battering at their restraints as shell after shell ripped through the barn. Kobold was as proficient as any of Stockburn's deputies. He reloaded and fired so fast there was hardly a pause between blasts. Charges ripped through the loft, through haystacks and empty stalls. He didn't concern himself with the stalls that were occupied. The frantic, pawing horses would make short work of anyone foolish enough to seek cover among them.

Not even the smallest potential hiding place was spared. Fifty-pound sacks of oats flew apart, sending a deluge of feed cascading to the stable floor. Old, partly rotten timbers overhead collapsed and hay came pouring down in waves.

Eventually running out of shells as well as out of targets, Kobold set the shotgun back on its shelf. It should take him only a minute or two to locate the body. He looked upward. Most likely it was lying up there, shattered by one or two loads of heavy buckshot from below.

It was a big axe, a man's axe, the double-bladed tool designed for splitting rails. It came flying through the air like a tomahawk. Kobold's eyes barely had time to go wide before it sliced through his right arm just above the elbow. The axe bounced off the opposite wall. The severed arm dropped to the floor, the shotgun still clenched in the now lifeless fist. Kobold gaped at it for another second.

Then he screamed.

Stockburn's eyes flicked in the direction of the cry. His expression did not alter. It rarely did. That granite visage was not capable of a broad range of expression.

Someone else heard the scream. High up in his opulent aerie Lahood found that his hands were beginning to shake. He poured himself a whiskey, hesitated, then made it a double and downed it straight if not quite neat. A slight trickle dribbled down his chin to stain the front of his immaculate shirt.

The Preacher emerged from the shadows and stepped over Kobold's writhing body. Pistol drawn, he headed toward the stable doors, ignoring the quivering, bleeding thing behind him.

At the last instant something made him hesitate. A slug splintered wood barely an inch from his face. Whirling, he threw himself back inside the stable, pressing his body against the interior wall. He took a deep breath, then tentatively peered out in an effort to pinpoint the location of the remaining deputy.

A second shot missed him by the same margin as its predecessor. Dropping to a crouch, he worked his way along the wall until he found a chink between two planks. He squinted through the narrow slit.

His range of vision was restricted, but he could still see most of the side street that fronted on the stable. There was the back wall of a clapboard building bordered by the skinny picket fence that was badly in need of a white-washing. There was the sickly apple tree in its yard, a watering trough, and across from it the windowless brick back wall of the town bank.

But of his assailant there was no sign. Whoever he was, he

was good. He'd managed to disappear himself as effectively as his quarry. An incautious step by either man now would be instantly fatal to the one making the move.

Eliminate the possibilities, use logic—a minute passed before the Preacher was nodding to himself. Rising, he stepped around the open door out into full view and raised his pistol. He fired six times, stitching a neat line the length of the horse trough. Water came pouring out through the half dozen punctures. It was clear at first but soon began to run crimson.

He headed toward the trough, reloading as he walked. The deputy's body floated within, the pistol still clutched in a dying hand. The Preacher's gaze came up.

Only one left now.

Stockburn had retreated back toward the warehouse, his expression inscrutable, his attitude implacable. He squinted up the street in the direction of the gunfire.

Then a figure stepped out from between the buildings. It moved to the middle of the street, apparently uninjured. There was something else in the middle of the street. A hat. The figure knelt to pick it up. The Preacher thoughtfully noted the position of the two holes. Then he dusted off the brim and set the hat back on his head, tugging it low over his eyes.

Fifty yards away, Stockburn was suddenly transformed. He grinned, an utterly humorless grin that did little to soften his appearance. He removed his own pistol and methodically checked the load. Then he stepped off the boardwalk out into the street. The fingers of his left hand were twisting and curling rapidly now while those of the right held the gun tightly. Fifty yards separated the two men. Fifty yards, and the bodies of the three deputies slain in the initial exchange.

He started up the street. Immediately the tall man moved to meet him. Both men measured their pace. There was nothing to disturb them, nothing to distract one man's attention from the other as they closed the distance between them. With infinite patience Stockburn was raising the muzzle of his own weapon. Each additional millimeter of arc he could cheat would enable him to get his shot off that much faster, would reduce the time he would have to spend to aim and fire.

And still his opponent's hand did not move, made no effort to match the Marshal's subtle shift in the attitude of his weapon. What the tall man did was raise his head slightly. For the first time the sun fully illuminated his face.

Stockburn met his eyes and for the first time the Marshal's expression underwent a radical change.

"You. *You!*"

He fired as fast as could have been expected to under the circumstances, confronted by that revelation, by the last face he could have been expected to see. Even with his surprise his hesitation was minuscule. His reaction was more instinct than calculation in any case. He fired with a speed born of years of practice at murder and killing.

It made no difference. The tall man got off five shots as one. The shells ripped an eight-inch circle into the Marshal's chest. Stockburn staggered, tried to aim, and fired a last time as the sixth shot blew the back of his head apart. He fell, unable to strike his opponent with even a final look of disbelief. The fingers of his left hand gave a last, repulsive twist.

Empty brass casings clattered on the ground as the Preacher emptied his cylinder. Calmly, matter-of-factly, he began to reload, his gaze still absorbed by the spread-eagled body of

Stockburn. Both the Marshal's hands were motionless, their nervous twitching stilled forever.

Closing the cylinder, he holstered the gun, pivoted, and strode across the now silent street toward his horse.

An ashen-faced Lahood stared out the second-story window, following the tall man's movements. In his right hand he held a long-barreled blue-black derringer. He raised the muzzle purposefully.

The Preacher put a foot in the stirrup and hesitated. Turning, he lifted his eyes to a particular window. The curtains behind it moved slightly. The report of the single shot was muffled by distance and glass. From his position the Preacher could not hear the thump of the body as it struck the thick Persian rug. He did not have to hear it.

Lahood had begun this day's work, and Lahood had finished it.

It was over.

Slipping smoothly into the saddle, the Preacher flicked the reins.

The buckboard came pounding into town, the slim figure seated on the bench refusing to ease back on the reins until it careened to a stop outside the bank. Some of Lahood's citizens spared it a passing glance. For the most part their attention was drawn to the numerous dead bodies that pimpled the street.

Megan jumped down from the buckboard. She had also seen the bodies and had scanned them anxiously. All were unknown to her. She altered her gaze to stare into the benumbed faces of the townsfolk. No one stared back at her.

"Where is he?"

No one had a reply. The shock of the morning's activities

was wearing off, but slowly. Even the mortician appeared too stunned to begin his chores.

She moved from figure to figure, confronting each and receiving only the same blank stares. Eventually she encountered the stout, familiar face of Jed Blankenship.

She grabbed him by his coat and demanded a response. "Where *is* he?"

The merchant blinked at her, then came out of the daze that had afflicted the rest of the citizenry. "Where is who, child?"

"The Preacher!"

"Ah. The Preacher." He looked down the main street and nodded. "He's gone."

"Gone where?"

Blankenship shrugged. "Who knows?"

Distraught, Megan turned away from him. Her eyes raked the street. It was full of citizens and corpses, but there was no sign of the tall figure she sought. Lips tight, she scrambled back aboard the wagon.

"Child!" Blankenship hurried after her, waving a restraining hand. She paused to gaze down at him. "Look at your horse, all lathered up like that. You ride her any more, you'll kill her. She needs rest. We all need a rest. The Preacher's gone, child."

He bestowed a fatherly smile on her, then turned purposefully back toward his emporium. Toting up the damage was going to take a lot of time and work, but he didn't mind. He was rid of his main competitor. When this day's accounting was amortized over the rest of the year, Jed Blankenship knew he'd be coming out far ahead.

He left Megan with the buckboard, feeling betrayed and near tears. After awhile she grew aware that the bodies filling the street no longer occupied everyone's attention. A few people had begun to stare at her.

She straightened, fighting back the tears. She was a Wheeler. Blankenship's words clung to her. "Gone?"

"No he's not," she murmured aloud. "Not really."

She unharnessed the mare, which was still breathing hard, and began to walk it back up the street. Halfway to the stable she stopped. Her eyes rose to the distant Sierra crest.

"Preacher!" she shouted. No more tears now, not ever. That was how it ought to be. It felt right. "I'm setting you free, Preacher! You hear me?"

A few of the townsfolk turned to eye her curiously. She had no trouble ignoring them. They didn't even exist. Only she existed, and the mountains.

"I'm setting you free!" Her voice fell slightly. "I love you, Preacher! Goodbye!" She patted the mare reassuringly on its neck. "He'll come back," she whispered to herself. "If I pray for him, he *will* come back. If I ever need him again, I'll just pray for a miracle."